The Way of Escape

Catherine Farnes

BJU PRESS
Greenville, South Carolina

Library of Congress Cataloging-in-Publication Data

Farnes, Catherine, 1964-
    The way of escape / Catherine Farnes.
        p. cm.
    Summary: Brenna is able to deal with the death of her parents and
her crushing load of grief when she is directed to the word of God
by her uncle, who is a preacher.
    ISBN 1-57924-454-8
    [1. Death—Fiction. 2. Grief—Fiction. 3. Uncles—Fiction.
4. Christian life—Fiction.] I. Title.

PZ7.F238265 Way 2000
[Fic]—dc21   00-047470

The Way of Escape

Editor: Gloria Repp
Project Editor: Debbie L. Parker
Designed by Duane A. Nichols
Cover illustration by Mary Ann Lumm

© 2000 Bob Jones University Press
Greenville, SC 29614

ISBN 1-57924-454-8

15   14   13   12   11   10   9   8   7   6   5   4   3   2   1

For Pastor Jim VanBuskirk,

who prayed with me to commit my life to Christ,

who baptized me in water,

who married John and me,

who dedicated my first baby,

whose "shoe leather Christianity" approach to applying

the Word of God sticks in my mind and leaves me

no room to make excuses,

and whose solid teaching

—and teaching to be solid—

at the beginning of my walk with God

has made all the difference.

Contents

Books by Catherine Farnes

The Rivers of Judah

Snow

Out of Hiding

The Way of Escape

Chapter 1

The last thing I wanted was dinner. But it was 6:00. We'd been driving all afternoon. We still had several hours of driving ahead of us, and the snow had let up a little. So we stopped to eat.

"Come on, Brenna," my Aunt Esther said to me. "Let's go find the ladies room. Your Uncle Ben'll get a table."

I nodded.

Aunt Esther put her arm over my shoulders and led me inside.

She was my dad's older brother's wife. Petite. Blond. Peaceful. She'd been with my younger brother, Connor, and me since the funeral a month ago. Helping us get our house in order and sold. Packing up the things we'd take with us and the things to be left in Grandpa's storage shed and sent to us a little at a time as he had opportunity to sort through them. Waiting on legalities. Trying to find out how we felt about things. But how we felt about things didn't really matter. There had been a will. Connor and I were to go with Uncle Ben and Aunt Esther. So we were going. To Colorado.

In the ladies room I washed my hands and stared at my face in the mirror. I had put my hair up and had worn my new dress for our going-away "party"—the pale pink dress I'd gotten for the funeral. We were Christians. Not like Uncle Ben and Aunt Esther, maybe. But we were Christians, and I believed that my parents were in heaven. No need to wear black about that. So I'd worn pink. Mom's favorite color. Earlier today, I had looked nice. Now? Too much crying and sitting in a car.

Aunt Esther stepped in behind me, gently pulled the clip out of my hair and then brushed it out with her brush. "You'll be more comfortable with your hair down," she said.

I nodded again. It occurred to me that I'd been doing a lot of that today. "Thanks." I leaned forward over the sink, filled my cupped hands with water, and splashed my face. Twice. Three times. "Okay," I said. I tossed a handful of paper towels into the garbage. "I'm ready now."

This time Aunt Esther nodded.

We found Uncle Ben, my cousin Nathan, and Connor— who'd been named after Dad—and joined them at the table the waitress had assigned to us. Uncle Ben closed his menu and laid it on the table.

"What are you going to have?" Aunt Esther asked him quietly as she sat beside him.

"I don't know," he said. "A cheeseburger, or something."

When the waitress came, Aunt Esther ordered for all of us, and then we sat and waited. In silence, until Uncle Ben said, "I hated leaving Mom and Dad like that."

"Everyone agrees it's best this way," Aunt Esther reminded him.

"Yeah," Connor said. "Everyone but Brenna and me."

Connor and I hadn't spent a lot of time with Dad's older brother and his family because we'd always lived so far apart. First they'd lived in Alaska. They'd been near us for a few months in Montana between churches. Then they'd gone to Colorado, where they still lived.

Where we would be living now.

Dad had always spoken with pride about his big brother, even though he didn't share Uncle Ben's desire to be such an "active" Christian. "Someone needs to be in the pews," he'd always say whenever he talked about his brother the pastor. "Otherwise, who would preachers preach at?" And that's what we'd been. Sometimes. Off and on. People in the pew.

I liked Uncle Ben and Aunt Esther well enough. And it was gracious of them to be willing to take Connor and me in. But I didn't want to go to Colorado. I didn't want to leave my grandparents. I didn't want to leave my friends. I didn't want to live in someone else's house. I didn't want to think about the pile of boxes Grandma and Grandpa had in their storage barn. Boxes of my stuff. Connor's stuff. Mom and Dad's stuff. Stuff that would be sold or given away later, when it wasn't so painful. I didn't want Mom and Dad to be . . .

I shut my eyes and willed myself not to cry again.

Things were the way they were.

"So you're a senior this year?" I asked Nathan.

"Yeah," he said. "And you're . . . ?"

"A sophomore," I said. "And Connor's a freshman."

Connor pulled the saltshaker toward him and slid it back and forth across the table in front of him. The noise annoyed me, but I didn't say anything.

Our food arrived. We ate it. Some of us. Some of it. Uncle Ben paid the bill, and we left.

Through the night, and through Wyoming, we drove. I tried to sleep but couldn't. At one point, Connor switched seats with Nathan and pulled me close to him. I let him, but I was too tired to acknowledge his comfort or return it. The night was dark and snowy and cold, and hardly anyone was out on the road. I suspected it had been a lot like this a month ago when Dad had driven his pickup off the road. He and Mom had gone into town to eat dinner and to buy Grandpa a birthday present.

Some birthday present he had gotten instead.

"There's an antelope," Aunt Esther said.

"I see it." Uncle Ben slowed the van, and I saw the back end of the animal as it bolted out of our headlight beams.

Connor held me more tightly, and I realized he was shaking. Or was it me that was shaking? I couldn't tell.

We drove.

"Are you all right?" Aunt Esther asked Uncle Ben. "Do you want me to drive?"

"I'm okay," he answered. "I was just thinking about a back-packing trip we took when I was about seventeen. Twenty-eight miles. From East Rosebud to Cooke City. Dad had planned to take the two of us boys, but then something came up at the ranch. He almost wasn't going to let us go. But he did, and it was the best thing for us." He laughed. "You know brothers. We had our fair share of arguments. But that trip . . ."

He didn't finish, and Aunt Esther didn't press him.

"Dad told me about that trip," Connor said, pulling away from me to lean forward. "He said you saw a bear."

"We did. Well, we didn't actually see it."

I wondered why Dad hadn't told me this story.

"We were in our tent," Uncle Ben was saying. "It was kind of a breezy night—you know how it is in the mountains. Branches were rubbing against the side of the tent all night. We'd hung our packs up in a tree a little ways away, and we hadn't brought any food into the tent, so I never expected any trouble from bears, though of course we knew they were in the area. Anyway, I guess it was about 2:00 in the morning when I woke up hearing something rubbing along the bottom of the tent. It didn't sound like any branches, and there was this smell. I can still remember that smell. Then I could hear breathing and grunting. I had a handgun, but I'd left it in my pile of clothes at the foot of my sleeping bag. I couldn't reach it, and I was too scared to move to get it. So I lay there. I don't think I was even breathing. Pretty soon I can see the snout pushing at the tent right by my face. The moon's up, and I can see what looks like this giant humped shadow on the side of the tent. Then I hear this whisper next to me, 'It's a Griz. We're going to die.' I barely managed a 'Shhh!'" Uncle Ben laughed. "I'd never been that scared before. Or since."

"What did you do?" I asked.

"I thought, 'God, I've never given You much thought up to now, and I'm not hypocritical enough to promise I'll give You more later, but I'm sure thinking about You at this moment. Please keep us safe.'"

"Well, what happened?" It was a stupid question. Uncle Ben didn't have any scars on his face, and he still had all his limbs. Obviously, God had kept them safe. I just wanted to know how.

"The bear sniffed around for a couple more minutes, and then just walked away," he said. "We could hear him over by the fire pit, crunching on something we must have dropped on the ground during dinner." He stayed quiet a moment. "It never left me alone that when He'd rescued us, God used the very thing that had drawn the grizzly to our camp."

Connor leaned back beside me and folded his arms across his stomach.

Don't say it, I thought. Uncle Ben's a pastor.

But Connor did say it. And coldly too. "You were just lucky. Why would God save you guys then and not save my parents in the accident?"

"I don't know, Connor," Uncle Ben answered. He sounded tired. "But—"

"Yeah, whatever," Connor muttered. "There isn't any God."

Uncle Ben left it alone.

"Did you see any tracks in the morning?" I asked. Anything to change the subject. "I mean, are you sure it was a griz?"

"Oh, yes," he said, "we saw tracks. It was definitely a griz."

"Scary," I said.

"At least someone enjoyed the backpacking food."

"That stuff is nasty," Nathan said.

We talked more about that trip, as well as about other memories we all had of Dad and Mom. We laughed a lot, cried a little, and faster than I would have imagined possible on this night, we were pulling into the driveway at Uncle Ben's house.

"You can have Rachel's room," Aunt Esther said as she walked up the stairs ahead of me. In each of her hands she held one of my suitcases. I was carrying two more. "I'm sorry it isn't completely packed up yet," she added. "Rachel will get the rest of her things when she comes home at Christmas." She pushed open the door that was immediately to the left at the top of the stairs and reached in to turn on the light.

On the stairs behind us, Uncle Ben and Connor were having a similar conversation about my cousin Judah's room.

Nathan's older sister and brother were both gone from home now. At college. Rachel was twenty. Four years older than me. And Judah was eighteen. I'd seen both of them at the funeral, but I hadn't spoken much to either one.

"The room'll be fine," I assured my aunt. As fine as any room that wasn't really mine could be. I walked in and set my bag on the bed. "Good night, Aunt Esther."

She came forward to lightly touch my cheek, then stepped out into the hallway again and pulled the door shut behind her.

As I got into some sweats and lay down on Rachel's bed, I wondered how long it would take for me to think of this room, of this place, of this life, as mine. I doubted I ever would. I turned out the light and shut my eyes. I'd unpack the rest of my things in the morning. It was late, and I had never before felt so tired.

Chapter 2

In the morning, since it was already a week into December, I asked Uncle Ben if I could wait to start school until after Winter Break. I thought it would help to not have to face all the challenges a new school would present until after I'd had some time to adjust to everything else. He spoke on the phone to the school counselor, who thought that would be fine since I had a decent GPA, and gave me permission.

Connor, however, wanted to start school as soon as he could get registered. "Like I want to sit around and think all day," he said.

That first week in Colorado, while Connor and Nathan were gone at school and Uncle Ben was working at the church, was awful. Long. Empty. Lonely. Aunt Esther tried to welcome me into her daily routine, and at the same time give me distance in case I wanted it. I didn't know what I wanted. I sat through half of her women's Bible study Tuesday morning thinking I'd rather be alone, and then spent all of Thursday afternoon by myself in Rachel's room wishing I had gone with Aunt Esther to the grocery store.

I had brought a picture of my parents in a pine frame. Sometimes it helped to look at it. Sometimes I wanted it face down on the table. And then I'd set it right again, angry at myself for being so weak.

That Thursday, I ran downstairs as soon as I heard Aunt Esther's car in the driveway and helped her unload and put away the groceries. Her kitchen was well organized, so it was easy to figure out where to put things. Mom's kitchen was like that too.

Or had been.

"When do you put up your tree?" I asked, shoving the thought of Mom's kitchen aside. "Or do you?"

She smiled. "We don't. Not because we think it's unchristian or anything. Our first house in Alaska was so small that we just didn't put one up. I guess we never got back into the habit. And besides that, we have a different tradition."

"What is it?" I asked.

"We started doing it when Rachel was eight," she said. "She asked Ben and me one night at dinner why we give each other gifts to celebrate Jesus' birthday. When people came to her birthday parties, they brought gifts for her, not for each other. Why wasn't it like that for Jesus' birthday?"

I smiled. Even if I'd had such a thought as a child, I certainly would not have mentioned it for fear that my parents might decide that we really didn't need presents for Christmas.

"We didn't really have a logical answer for her except that it's celebrating the fact that the Magi brought gifts for Jesus," Aunt Esther continued. "She thought about that for a few days, and then on another night she announced that she didn't want to get Christmas presents anymore. She wanted us to take the money we would have spent on gifts for her and give it to missions—or something like that—as a present to Jesus that would make Him happy."

"Wow," I said. "I'm impressed."

Aunt Esther nodded. "So were Ben and I."

"So that's what you do now?"

"Yes."

"The boys didn't mind?"

"No," she said. Then she laughed a little. "Well, they adjusted. They still got presents from their grandparents and their aunts and uncles. And I always made each of them something, or we got them something they needed anyway and wrapped it up."

"So what do you do with the presents you do get, since you don't put up a tree?"

"We set up a manger scene on a table and put the gifts on the floor in front of it."

"That sounds nice," I said. In a way, I was relieved that we wouldn't be putting up a tree. If Christmas was different here, it might not make me think so much of Christmas at home. "When do you set it up?"

"In a week or so," she said. She put the last package of pasta in the cupboard and then turned to look at me. "Would you like a tree, Brenna?"

"No," I said quickly. "No."

Aunt Esther walked across the room to hug me. "This is a hard time of year to . . ." Her embrace was warm, and caring, and sincere, so I let myself lean into her and cry. I didn't pull away from her until I heard footsteps on the porch. Nathan and Connor arriving home from school. Or Uncle Ben, home early from the church. Either way, I wanted to be done blubbering like a baby by the time they walked through the house and into the kitchen. Aunt Esther pushed the hair back from my face and handed me a tissue for my eyes.

"Thanks," I told her. For more than the tissue.

It was Uncle Ben. He hugged his wife first thing when he came into the kitchen, and then gave me a gentle squeeze of the shoulder. He loosened his tie as he sat down at the table and began going through his mail.

He looked so much like my father. Brown hair. Brown eyes. Uncle Ben's hair was cut a little shorter than Dad's had been—a little neater—and his face showed a little more age than Dad's had. More than the two years' worth that separated them. I supposed that being a pastor could be quite a bit more stressful in some ways than working with horses, which is what Dad had done. It certainly had been stressful for Uncle Ben a couple of years back when that boy in Alaska had drowned. I knew that. And bad for Judah too. I remembered him waking up screaming in the middle of the night once when all of us kids were sleeping on the living room floor at Grandpa and Grandma's. He'd dreamed about when they'd found the body. I wondered if they'd ever made peace with that family. Probably not. How could there be peace with something like that between people?

Horses are difficult, Dad would always say, but a guy can understand them. Not people. And all that right and wrong. No, sir. Ben's crazy.

"Some hot chocolate, Brenna?"

I smiled up at Aunt Esther and nodded. "How was your day today?" I asked Uncle Ben.

He put down the letter he'd been skimming and looked at me. He seemed to be somewhat surprised by the question. "Thursdays," he said, "I spend all day in counseling sessions."

I grimaced. That didn't sound like much fun. A bunch of people, one right after the other, whining and complaining about everything that was wrong with their lives, and probably expecting Uncle Ben to have the miracle solution.

"This time of year," he said, "people are either a little more depressed than usual, or more optimistic. The holiday roller coaster. I had more of the latter than the former today, so I'd have to say it was a good day."

It couldn't have been that good, I thought. He looked discouraged. And drained. Of course, his brother had died, and he had just come home with two extra teenagers to care for. I wondered if he had anyone to go to for counseling.

"What kinds of things do people come to you for counseling for?" I asked him.

"All sorts of things," he said. "There's pre-marriage counseling. Marriage counseling. People in the middle of divorce. People struggling with sin. Parents and kids trying to work through issues. Eating disorders. Financial advice. Depression." He shrugged. "You name it, I figure I've dealt with it at some point or other."

"Do you always have an answer for them?"

He smiled as he shook his head. "I always have the Word of God, though, and it does."

I nodded politely. Of course he'd say that. But I had to wonder if it really did. Sure, it could tell you how to get to heaven, how to live a good life, and how to avoid a miserable one. But could it really tell me why my parents couldn't have missed that deer on the highway? Could it really tell me how I was supposed to move on from here with any sort of peace?

I didn't think so.

And I didn't ask Uncle Ben.

Half an hour passed before we heard Connor and Nathan at the front door, home from school. Nathan entered the kitchen first and muttered a greeting to his parents and me. He grabbed a soda from the refrigerator and hurried upstairs to his room. His door slammed hard as Connor came in and sat at the table beside me. He glanced toward the stairs and asked Uncle Ben if Nathan was always so pleasant.

Uncle Ben grinned. "Not always."

"Must have had a bad day," Aunt Esther said.

I had the feeling that Connor knew exactly what had been bad about Nathan's day. And not only that. I suspected that he'd had something to do with it. He was sitting slightly slouched in his chair, smugly trying to keep one of his crooked grins from completely overtaking his features. His classic *I sure got under his skin this time* posture. A posture I recognized from far too much personal exposure to it.

My little brother was, and always had been, a bully. He liked to have the advantage, and if there wasn't one readily to be had, he'd create one. He'd tease. He'd hide things. He'd make you think he knew or that he had something you wanted. And when you fell for it, he'd sit there very much as he was sitting at Uncle Ben and Aunt Esther's table now. Gloating. Proud of himself. Absolutely pleased with what he thought was his incredible ingenuity.

"What did you do?" I asked him.

"Nothing," he said . . . and I knew right then that he was lying. It was his tone of voice. The indignant way he'd said it. It had deceived Mom and Dad more than once, but it did not deceive me.

"Connor, what did you do?"

My questioning seemed to be exactly what Connor had been hoping for. He watched Uncle Ben and Aunt Esther until he knew he had their attention, and then he said, "I said something about this girl at school. Turns out she's a close friend of Nathan's."

I sighed and shook my head. "Oh, Connor."

"And let me guess," Uncle Ben said. "Your comment wasn't complimentary?"

Connor shrugged. "I just mentioned the color of her hair."

"I see," said Uncle Ben.

I could feel tension from Uncle Ben and Aunt Esther, and Connor's abundant disrespect, but the conversation had lost me. The color of her hair? What could possibly be offensive about mentioning the color of someone's hair? Unless . . . I giggled. "What? Is Nathan's friend a punk rocker, or something?"

Instantly I regretted my amusement.

Uncle Ben turned his full attention to me, and it was not appreciative. "No, Brenna," he said quietly. "His friend is—"

"An albino!" Connor finished.

A . . . what?

"An albino," Connor repeated in answer to my unspoken question. "You know, like the sacred white buffalo of the—"

"That will do."

I didn't know if it was Uncle Ben's tone, or his glare, or just the fact that Connor didn't yet know how far he could or should dare to push the man. Whatever it was, it worked. Connor snapped his mouth shut and even seemed to sit up a little straighter.

Uncle Ben spoke to me, but he kept looking at Connor. "Stephanie is an albino, Brenna," he said. "That means she has no pigment in her skin or hair, and that she is legally blind because of the lack of pigment in one of the layers of the eye." Nothing changed in Uncle Ben's voice or expression, but I knew his next words were for Connor. "She is a human being, just like you, and will be respected as such by everyone in this house."

This is what I had most feared about coming to live with Uncle Ben and Aunt Esther. They would have tougher standards than Mom and Dad, and they would expect us to live by them because we were in their house. Connor would never go for that. He had barely managed to comply with Dad's rules.

I stiffened in my chair for a *You're not my father, so get off my back* tirade from Connor.

And sure enough, it came.

Chapter 3

An almost inaudible knock at Rachel's bedroom door late Saturday night startled me out of the half-sleep I'd worked very hard to achieve. I got out of the bed, pulled on my robe, and walked across the room to turn on a light and open the door.

Connor hurried past me and sat on the edge of the bed. "We need to talk," he said.

I closed the door. "Now?"

"Now."

"All right." I sat beside him. "So talk."

"Did Uncle Ben invite you to join them for church tomorrow?"

I nodded. "Well, Aunt Esther did."

"We're not going. He can't make us go, and we're not going to."

I stared at him. "I don't remember asking you to make that decision for me, Connor."

"You want to go?"

"No. Maybe. I don't know."

"We're not going," he said again. "That's it."

I found the end of the belt at my waist and started rolling it. Pink. Thick. Soft. "I can go if I want to."

He thought about that for only a second. "Listen, we have to stick together here, or, the next thing you know, we'll be singing in the choir."

I laughed. "Uncle Ben's church doesn't have a choir."

"You know what I mean."

Yes. I knew what he meant.

"Why don't they have a choir?"

"Oh, how would I know? I just remember Rachel writing to me that they didn't have one here." I quit playing with the end of my belt. Actually, it was Mom's belt. Mom's robe. I had it only because I'd borrowed it a couple of days before the accident, and it had still been in my room when Aunt Esther was helping me pack my things before we left. "We're living in their house now, Connor, and they aren't our enemies. Why do we have to 'stick together' against them?"

"Against going to church," he said, enunciating each word as if I were some sort of imbecile. "I don't believe in God—"

"So you keep saying. But Mom and Dad raised us to—"

"—and I'm not going to sit in some stupid church service every week just because we had to come live here with our uncle the pastor." He glared at me. "You don't still believe all that God stuff, do you, Bren? After what's happened?"

"I believe in God," I assured him.

"Then you're stupid."

For several minutes, neither of us moved nor spoke. Connor fumed. I squinted my eyes shut and tried to ignore the sudden tightening in my stomach. Finally, only because I couldn't stand the silence, I said, "All right. I'll stick with you on this one. This time."

And that's exactly what I did.

I announced to Aunt Esther over a plateful of her delicious applesauce pancakes that maybe we'd go with them next Sunday, but not today, thanks. Connor winked at me across the table when he knew nobody would see.

We'd done it.

We'd stuck together against going to church and had prevailed.

But it hadn't even been a fight. Uncle Ben had simply nodded his tolerance of our decision for this week, saying that we'd talk the subject through more thoroughly later. Somehow, I would have preferred a fight. Maybe then I'd have been able to feel something other than miserable.

Connor and I sat in the den watching who knew what on television for nearly three hours. When I stood up and turned it off, Connor didn't even notice.

"We should have gone to church," I said. "Dad and Mom would want us to, I'm sure. And even if they didn't care so much about that, they'd definitely want us to respect Uncle Ben and Aunt Esther." Tears pushed their way out, and I didn't fight them. "We should have gone with them." I turned to look at Connor, who was still sitting on the couch. "Even if we didn't want to."

Though his initial expression was one of disgust—because I was crying again?—he quickly replaced it with a more sympathetic one. "I guess I just wanted to see if they'd try to make us. You know. 'Church will be attended by everyone in this house.' Like not making fun of Nathan's friend."

"Well, they didn't."

"No. They didn't." He stood up and walked across the room to the stereo cabinet. "But they still might." He ran his finger along the edges of several CD cases as he skimmed the titles. "There is not one piece of decent music in this place."

"What were you expecting?"

"Equal time, maybe—for God stuff and real stuff."

"I guess Uncle Ben figures the God stuff *is* the real stuff."

"Apparently. I'm going to call Grandpa and have him send my music. I forgot to pack it."

I wondered if Uncle Ben would put up with my brother's favorite bands pulsing through the walls of his house. I suspected not but didn't say so to Connor. He seemed to be looking for issues to build up and magnify between himself and our uncle, and I wasn't about to encourage that. It was bad enough that Mom and Dad were gone and that we'd been uprooted and moved halfway across the country to live with relatives we really didn't know. Why stir in conflict?

"I'm going to go start lunch," I said. "They should be getting home soon."

Connor put on a ridiculous exaggerated smile. "Oh goodie."

"Connor . . ." I shook my head and walked out of the room. It would be pointless to try to reason with him. He'd decided to be angry and bitter and sarcastic, and that's what he would be until something smacked him out of it. I only hoped that that *something* would come soon, and that Uncle Ben would be able to keep his calm and survive in the meantime—because Connor was making it abundantly clear that he had no intention of keeping his.

Hoping I wasn't using too many ingredients that Aunt Esther had bought with a specific meal in mind, I put together a chicken casserole and set it in the oven to bake. I cleaned up the dishes I'd used, and I then sat at the table to write a list of things I definitely wanted Grandpa to send. Our family scrapbook. My hiking boots. The necklace Dad had given me for Christmas last year that I'd kept in Mom's jewelry box.

Christmas. How everything had changed between the one I'd celebrated last year and the one I'd be observing in less than three weeks.

I finished my list for Grandpa and then wrote a letter to accompany it. How are you doing, Grandpa? And Grandma . . . how is she? How are the horses? Are the cattle surviving the winter all right? Who have you hired to help with the place now that Dad is gone? I can't say how things are here for sure yet. I miss you. Love, Brenna. It wasn't much of a letter. I knew that. But my grandparents would understand.

Connor came into the kitchen and sat beside me just as I sealed the envelope and flipped it over to address it. He watched me print Grandpa's name, Mr. Jesse Ewen, and then asked, "Did you tell him to send my music?"

"Do it yourself," I muttered.

"Okay. If you're going to be that way." He yanked the envelope out from underneath my left hand, grabbed the pen from my right hand, and wrote *Hi, Grandpa, Can you send me some of my CDs? I need something to listen to besides hymns. Connor* on the back of the envelope. Then he slid it back to me. "There. I did it myself."

"Yeah. And I'm sure Grandpa will be honored by the effort you put into it."

"He'll understand," Connor said. "He doesn't like hymns any more than I do."

"Oh, forget it." I finished addressing the envelope and set it on top of Aunt Esther's pile of outgoing mail. Grandpa might not like hymns, I reflected, but he didn't appreciate Connor's music, either. And he was very proud of Uncle Ben. His oldest son. Maybe he would be irritated enough by Connor's disrespect to disregard his request for a while. Maybe he would ignore it altogether. Connor could definitely stand to hear a good hymn or two. Even Grandpa would think so.

"Lunch smells good," Connor said. "What did you make?"

"Mom's chicken casserole."

"Hm." He followed one of the curves of wood grain on the tabletop with his fingertip. "I guess it's your chicken casserole now."

I stood to tell him to be quiet. It was Mom's recipe, and it always would be. Why did he have to be such a jerk, anyway? I knew Mom was gone. He didn't have to remind me like that.

But I didn't get a chance to say anything or even to open my mouth because Uncle Ben, Aunt Esther, and Nathan came in the front door. I went to the oven and pretended to be checking on lunch so that they wouldn't see how ready I was for tears.

Again.

When would I be able to get through a day without either crying or trying hard not to, I wondered. When?

Aunt Esther set her purse on the table and walked up behind me. "The food smells wonderful, Brenna," she said quietly. And then she just stood there. Right beside me. After a moment, she placed her hand over mine on the oven handle. "Your mother's recipe?"

I nodded.

"Maybe, when a bit more time has gone by, you can share it with me."

How was it that she'd known exactly what to say to validate my feelings? To let me know she understood and was there for me? And how had she been able to guess so accurately at what was bothering me?

Maybe my feelings were normal, and I shouldn't be so frustrated by them.

"I'd be happy to share it with you," I told her. "In fact, I asked Grandpa to send me her whole recipe book—the one she put together herself. I'll show it to you."

"I'd like that," she said.

"Maybe we could, you know, cook out of it together sometime."

Aunt Esther squeezed my hand and nodded. "I'd like that too."

Nathan stepped between us just then and pulled the oven door open. "I'm starved," he said, "and this smells excellent." He stood up straight and pushed the oven door shut again. "When do we eat?"

"Right now," I said.

"Great." Nathan opened the cupboard beside the stove and pulled out a stack of plates. "Dad preached long today."

"Oh, and I missed it," said Connor from his place at the table behind us.

Aunt Esther stiffened a little beside me, but she said nothing.

Uncle Ben, however, laughed. "Let me grab my notes. I'll preach it again now. Just for you."

"That's okay," Connor said. I could tell by his tone that he was grinning, but not whether it was genuine. "We're about to eat, and it's rude to talk with your mouth full. Even about God."

"He's right, Dad," Nathan said.

Uncle Ben watched with interest as I brought the casserole dish to the table and set it down. "Hm," he said. "So he is."

Chapter 4

During the three weeks that led up to Christmas, my mind churned through and spit out so many different emotions only to scoop them back up again that I thought I would drive myself and everyone around me crazy. Hours seemed to take years to pass when I was awake and never lasted long enough during sleep. I'd cry. Then I'd get angry. Then I'd catch myself enjoying a fond memory and start the cycle all over again. I'd talk to Aunt Esther sometimes, but mostly I shut myself away from her. Connor kept telling me to get a grip, and I kept telling him to leave me alone.

It was the worst three weeks of my life.

I missed Mom. And Dad. And home. I wanted my brother to be a strength to me, and all he was, was bitter and mean. I wanted to have faith in God, but all I could think was that He'd been sitting up on His throne when Mom and Dad had come around the corner in their truck to meet that deer. He could have inspired the deer to stay away. He could have given Mom one of those intuitions of hers to stay home that night instead of heading into town. He could have . . .

Well, He could have done any number of things. Or all of them. He's God.

But He'd done nothing.

I knew that I was supposed to be able to take refuge in Him. To look to Him to piece it all back together for good. To thank Him for Jesus' work on the cross that allowed me to know with a certainty that my parents were in heaven now, and that I'd be there too one day.

I knew all of that. But it was hard to do. For me, and even more so for Connor. So much so that I'd begun to worry for him. Had he really stopped believing in God as he'd been claiming? Had he ever believed in Him in the first place?

I realized that I really didn't know.

Everything seemed to have become so convoluted.

And it didn't look as if it was going to unravel any time soon. I walked into the kitchen for a glass of milk very late on the Thursday night three days before Christmas and found my uncle at the table. He'd fallen asleep with a pen still in his hand and his Bible and unfinished sermon notes in front of him.

I giggled a little.

If the sermon he was working on had put him to sleep . . .

I didn't laugh for long, though. The clock on the stove said 2:14. Uncle Ben and Aunt Esther always went to bed at a reasonable hour. They had to now that they were getting older, they said. And I'd been watching television when they'd gone up that night. So why was Uncle Ben downstairs at 2:00 in the morning?

I placed my hand lightly on his shoulder. "Uncle Ben?"

He startled awake, looked up at me, and then leaned forward to press at his eyes with the heels of his hands. "What time is it?"

I told him.

"Couldn't sleep?" he asked me.

"Not really."

He sat back in his chair again. "Neither could I."

I sat in the chair beside his. "Is that Sunday's sermon?"

"This?" He lifted the note pad from the table, studied it for a moment, and then set it back down. "Not yet."

"Not captivating enough?" I grinned.

"Apparently not."

We laughed quietly together for a second or two and then went silent. When several minutes had passed and Uncle Ben still hadn't moved to head upstairs, I ventured, "Would you like something to drink? I could make some hot tea."

"Sure, Brenna. Thank you."

After I'd gotten two cups down, the tea bags, a spoon, and the sugar, I sat down to wait for the water to boil and the kettle to whistle. "Are you looking forward to having Judah and Rachel home tomorrow?"

"Yes."

"Did you hear back from that family in Alaska?" I asked. "Are they still coming?"

Uncle Ben's expression clouded slightly, and he looked away from me toward the dark window. "Yes. Tuesday."

They'd gotten a call a couple of weeks ago from one of the families in their church in Alaska . . . how about if we come see you for Christmas? I'd have thought that they'd be excited about seeing old friends, but both Uncle Ben and Aunt Esther, and even Nathan, seemed always to get quiet when the subject came up. I supposed it had something to do with that boy's drowning.

Painful memories.

I waited for Uncle Ben to look at me again. "Is that what was keeping you up?"

"No," he said. "I was thinking about Connor."

"He's obnoxious. It's just his way of griev—"

Uncle Ben smiled. "Not your brother. Mine."

"Oh."

We went silent again. After a while, the kettle whistled. I got up, fixed the tea, brought the cups to the table, and sat back down. Neither of us touched our cups.

"Connor and I hadn't spent a lot of time together since we both grew up and had our separate lives," Uncle Ben said. "But, I don't know, I guess I didn't think about it much because I could always pick up the phone and talk to him or get on a plane to Montana. His life was busy. My life was busy." He stirred a couple teaspoons of sugar into his tea and wrapped his hands around the warm cup. "I can't pick up the phone anymore, and there're things I didn't say."

I nodded. "There are things I didn't say, Uncle Ben, and we lived in the same house." I felt tears at my eyes and moved to push them away before Uncle Ben noticed, but I stopped because there were tears at his eyes too.

"I know from counseling, and from other experiences of my own," he said, "that it's normal to feel this way." He looked right at me. "And it can be tempting to let ourselves get lost in grief. Do you want to know what the Bible says about temptation?"

I shrugged and then nodded. I guess.

He picked up his Bible and flipped through the pages at the back. "Well, it says a lot of things, actually. But here's the verse I'm thinking of." He read, *"There hath no temptation taken you but such as is common to man: but God is faithful, who will not suffer you to be tempted above that ye are able; but will with the temptation also make a way to escape, that ye may be able to bear it."*

I kept looking at him but didn't say anything. How was I supposed to escape from the fact that my parents were gone? They were gone and always would be. I could never "escape" back to the time when they weren't. Slowly, I raised my cup and took a sip of my tea. I'd let it steep too long. It had gone bitter. But it didn't matter. I wasn't thirsty anyway. "Uncle Ben?"

"Yeah?"

"Why did . . . why didn't . . . why did God let this happen?"

He slid his chair right up next to mine and took both of my hands in both of his. "Sweetie, I don't have that answer."

"But the Bible does . . . that's what you said, right? It has the answers?" Even as I asked, though, I couldn't help wondering if all the answers that the Bible had would make as little sense as the verse he'd just read to me.

"It has the answer in this respect," he said. "The Bible tells me that our days are in God's hand. That death happens to all of us at some point or another, in one way or another, as a result of the curse. And that God is over all of it."

"And that means . . . ?"

"God knew the accident was going to happen," he said. "The way I see it, He knew about it before any of us were born. He's all-powerful, so He could have prevented it. I believe He does protect us. But at some point, every person has a time to die."

"So you're saying it was Mom and Dad's time?"

"I'm saying," he said, "that if it hadn't been . . . yes, Brenna. I guess that's what I'm saying."

"You guess?"

"In my mind, the way I perceive and understand things as a man, as a human being without the divine knowledge that God has, it makes no sense to me that it would ever be someone's time to die when he was young. When he still had kids to raise. A whole life to live. But God knows the end from the beginning, and He understands in a way that I can't." Uncle Ben's hold on my hands tightened as he stared more intensely at me. "I've counseled people who sat in my office and tried to rationalize death. Well, God let so-and-so die now because He knew that she'd turn away from her faith later. Or, He let my husband die first because He knew that he'd never survive my death if I went first. Things like that. But I can't do that. Or let me say it this way. I find no comfort in that because it's all speculation."

"So what do you find comfort in?" I asked him. I'd barely managed the voice for it, but we were face to face. I knew he'd heard me.

"God has proven Himself trustworthy to me in things I can see and understand."

"So?"

"So, when something plows over me that I can't understand, I know He'll be just as trustworthy. The fact that I can't see the whole equation doesn't change who God is."

I gently pulled my hands out of his grasp to wipe my eyes. Tears again. Lots of them. "But you still don't have the answer to *why?*"

"I don't need that answer, Brenna." He stood up, pushed his chair back enough so that he could step by it, and grabbed the box of tissues off the counter. As he handed it to me, he sat down again. "I can't lie to you. I'm a human being. Things make more sense to me and are easier to digest when I can see whether it was five and five that made ten or three and three four. But, if we know that ten is the right answer because the mathematician who worked the equation doesn't make mistakes, then—"

"I see what you're saying," I said. "But feelings still have to be lived with."

"Yes. They do. And that's what keeps us up at night."

"Even you," I said.

He squinted at me, clearly surprised by the fact that I was surprised by the fact that he'd been up nights struggling.

I watched him get stiffly out of his chair, return it to its spot at the table, and place his full cup of tea in the sink. Perhaps I should have said *Especially you* instead of *Even you.* Who else but a pastor would be asked at 2:00 in the morning why God had allowed a tragedy to happen and actually be expected to answer?

Chapter 5

Saturday morning, the day before Christmas Eve, was the last rehearsal before the Family Christmas Program, so Connor and I rode to church with our cousin Judah. I suspected that he'd offered to take us along with him solely to give his father a reprieve from Connor's unrelenting iciness about having to go. Aunt Esther had asked all of us to go and help the youth pastor set up chairs, and Connor had been pouting aloud all morning. It had worn on everyone.

"I'm going to stop by and pick up a friend of mine," Judah said as he backed his Jeep out of the driveway. "Rebekah. Is that all right?"

"Sure," I said. I'd met Rebekah and had talked with her when she'd come with her mother to the Women's Christmas Fellowship that Aunt Esther had hosted at the house, and I'd seen her again each time I'd gone to church. She seemed nice enough. Caring. "It's fine with me."

"What if it isn't fine with me?" Connor asked.

Judah laughed a little. "I guess you'll just have to live with it," he said, "because you're in my car and that's where it's going."

"Like father like son," Connor muttered.

"That's not an insult." Judah put the Jeep in gear and headed slowly up Bethel Road. Snow was falling on a strong west wind in huge wet flakes. Visibility was very poor, and the roads were icy underneath the new snow because the old snow had melted in yesterday's afternoon sun and had refrozen after dark.

"Were the roads like this all the way across South Dakota and Wyoming?" I asked Judah.

"Pretty much," he said. "But it was worth it to get home for Christmas."

I turned to my window and looked at my reflection against a background of swirling white.

Home for Christmas.

My shoulders tensed against the sudden flush in my cheeks as I tried to shove the sentiment aside, along with everything it brought to my mind. But I was powerless against the force of the emotion, and I started to cry. Silently, at first, and then in embarrassing but undeniable sobs.

Beside me, Connor groaned and mumbled. "Here she goes again."

In front of me, Judah apologized.

Connor sulked. Judah drove. I cried.

Judah left the motor running and the heater blowing when he got out at Rebekah's house. I watched him through my tears, the snow, and the windshield wipers scraping back and forth across the glass. He hurried up the sidewalk, waited at the door for a moment with his hands shoved in his pockets, received and returned a hug from Mrs. Cahill, and then another one from Rebekah. He held her arm as they approached the Jeep and smiled at something she said.

I wiped at my eyes with my gloved hands and refused the rest of my tears. It was one thing to blubber like an idiot in front of my brother and my cousin, but I barely knew Rebekah.

Besides, she and Judah should be allowed to enjoy seeing one another since they hadn't in a while. Nathan had told me that they weren't officially dating because Judah was away at school, but nobody had any doubts about the future of their relationship.

Judah opened the front passenger door for Rebekah and held her arm while she climbed up and inside. When he shut the door and was walking around the front of the Jeep, she said, "I hate getting into this thing in a skirt!" Then she smiled at Connor and at me. "Hi, Brenna," she said. "I'm glad you decided to come help, Connor. Pastor Dave will really appreciate it."

"It was decided for me," he said. "Today and every stupid Sunday from now on until I leave."

"Oh." Rebekah's expression revealed her complete lack of anything to say. She did manage another *Oh* as Judah climbed in and pulled his door shut, and then hurried to redirect her full attention to him. How are your classes? How's your job? Are you exhausted from the drive yesterday? It's good to see you. I'm thinking about moving into my own place. Did I tell you that already?

Judah replied to everything Rebekah said, but I could tell by the way he kept glancing over his shoulder at Connor and me that he felt awkward about the casual conversation. After all, he knew that Connor was angry enough to spit and that I'd just dried up seven blocks worth of crying.

When we arrived at the church, Judah came around to open Rebekah's door and then stepped back and opened mine. "Are you all right?" he asked me. "I'm really sorry; I didn't—"

I shook my head. "It wasn't your fault. I'm sure someone will mention Christmas. How can they not? That's what set me off. Better to fall apart in the car than in front of everyone!" I could just envision it. The kids' choir would be up on the platform singing "We Wish You a Merry Christmas" and there I'd be, in the middle of a whole group of teens, with the options of running out of the sanctuary with my hand over my mouth or staying put and trying to strangle back my tears without making too much noise. "You probably did me a favor," I told Judah with a smile. The first genuine one of the morning.

Uncle Ben arrived at the church shortly after we did. He went to the pulpit to read part of the Christmas story out of the book of Luke and to coordinate the mini-sermon he would be doing with the silent action of the play continuing on behind him. They had to run through it two or three times before they managed to finish at the same time, but nobody minded. Uncle Ben's words had the rapt attention of everyone in the place.

Even my brother's, I suspected, though he was doing everything he could think of to make it appear that he was bored. Cracking his knuckles. Slouching in his chair. Staring up at the ceiling lights. Banging his heel against the metal bar at the bottom of his chair.

I leaned close to him and whispered, "He's a good speaker. You've got to at least give him that."

"I don't have to give him anything," he whispered back and then returned to his brooding.

I survived the entire rehearsal without crying again, including several attempts afterwards by well-meaning people to encourage me.

"We'll be praying for you, honey."

"It's such a difficult time of year when you've had a loss."

"Keep looking to God."

I nodded politely and thanked them for their concern because I did appreciate it. But I would have preferred to have been left alone. Thankfully, Rebekah and Stephanie—Nathan's friend—rescued me. They pulled me into Uncle Ben's office and shut the door.

"You looked pretty uncomfortable," Rebekah said.

I nodded.

"They're only trying to help," Stephanie said.

"I know."

"Are you all right?"

I shrugged. "Yeah. Yeah. I mean, you know. As all right as I'm going to be."

The three of us sat in the office in silence for a while until Stephanie asked Rebekah if she'd gotten all her Christmas shopping done.

Christmas shopping!

I had been so preoccupied with dreading Christmas that it hadn't even occurred to me to buy gifts—and it was the day before Christmas Eve.

"You guys," I said, "I . . . I don't have anything for anyone. I . . . I can't believe I didn't—"

Rebekah stepped toward me and hugged me. "You know what? I have to run to the mall today and pick up a couple of last minute things. Why don't you come with me? I'd like the company, and—"

I smiled. "And you know what my aunt and uncle and Judah, Nathan, and Rachel would like."

She backed away from me and grinned. "I could probably make some pretty good guesses." Then she turned to Stephanie. "Why don't you come with us? I'll have Judah drop us off at my house for my car, and we can spend the afternoon together."

"I'll ask my parents," Stephanie said. "Sounds fun."

"Yeah, it does," I agreed. "Thanks."

I didn't have a lot of money, but after a couple of hours of careful shopping I'd found something small and unique for each of my cousins and Uncle Ben and Aunt Esther, and even something for Connor. I had each of the gifts wrapped and labeled at the mall, and I chose a card to send to my grandparents. I felt horrible that I hadn't sent cards to any of my friends back home and said so to Rebekah as we were driving back to the house.

"You can call them," she suggested. "I'm sure they understand that things are hard on you right now."

"I hope so," I said. But I had to wonder. The town we'd lived in near Grandpa and Grandma's ranch was small. There were only eight kids in my grade, and I'd known all of them since before kindergarten. Through the years, I had been both best friend and worst enemy to each of them. More than once. We all knew everything there was to know about one another. We were close, but defensive. Connor had been in basically the same predicament, except that his class had twelve kids and he'd had one constant friend, Kody Urstaad.

I wondered if I would ever have a friendship like that—one I could count on no matter what.

I hoped so.

When Rebekah pulled into Uncle Ben's driveway, Stephanie opened her door and jumped out of the car before I'd even unbuckled my seat belt. "I'll walk you in," she said.

"Me too," said Rebekah.

I smiled at her eagerness to see Judah again. "What a surprise!"

The house was quiet when the three of us piled onto the rug inside the front door to take off our boots. Aunt Esther was rearranging the candles she had placed on the mantel. Connor was talking on the telephone. Rachel was reading a magazine. And Judah and Nathan were sitting on opposite ends of the coffee table, engrossed in a game of chess. They both managed to acknowledge Rebekah and Stephanie when the girls sat next to them on either side of the table, but barely.

I hurried to hide my packages among the others beneath the painted wooden stable and its painted wooden cast of characters and then followed Aunt Esther to the kitchen. "Where's Uncle Ben?" I asked her.

"Upstairs." She handed a knife to me along with a bundle of celery. "Hoping to sleep off a headache."

I remembered her telling me the same thing a couple of days earlier. And another time a few days before that. "He gets a lot of those."

She nodded. "He hasn't been sleeping well."

"I guess that doesn't surprise me."

"It's these Ewen men and stress," she said. "It gets to them physically. Ben gets headaches. Judah gets sick to his stomach. Your grandfather—"

"Twitches his knee up and down for hours on end." I laughed. "You're right. Dad can't sit still when he's stressed about something. Mom just hands him her honey-do list, and he goes at it." The knife beat rhythmically against the plastic cutting board as I sliced the celery. "Or did."

Aunt Esther looked cautiously at me, probably waiting to make sure I wasn't going to start crying. When I didn't, she said, "Nathan just gets angry."

"So does Connor." I directed the chopped celery into a glass bowl with the blade of my knife. "Are we having turkey for Christmas dinner?"

"Ham."

That's what we'd always had at home too. "Are people coming over?"

"Yes." Aunt Esther smiled. "Stephanie and her parents. Rebekah and her parents. And another family from church . . . have you met the Kramer boys? Tony and Michael?"

I shook my head. "No."

"I guess you wouldn't have met Michael yet. He's older, Rachel's age, and has been away at school. Tony's still home, though. He's a senior this year."

"Oh," I said. "Sounds like we'll have a full house."

"We always do on holidays," she said. "It's one of those things about Ben's . . ." Slowly, her mouth closed and her knife went still. "Brenna," she said, "I didn't even think to talk to you and Connor about Christmas dinner. You'd probably rather not have all kinds of people around. How could I have been so careless?" She set her knife down, dried her hands on a towel, and walked out of the room toward the hallway. "I'll call them and—"

I ran up behind her and grabbed her arm. "Aunt Esther, it's okay. It'll be fine."

She looked at me, obviously uncertain. "What about Connor?"

I laughed. "He'll find something to complain about either way."

Her expression relaxed. A little.

"Really," I said. "Don't change your plans."

"I'll talk to Connor," she said. "And your Uncle Ben."

"At different times, I hope?"

She considered the question for several seconds. "Why?"

I put my arm over her shoulder and led her back into the kitchen. "Because Connor will allow Uncle Ben to give his opinion first and then disagree just because. And then your poor husband will be upstairs sleeping away another headache while my brother—"

"Ah. Understood." She smiled. "I'll make sure they're not even in earshot of each other!"

Chapter 6

Christmas Day after dinner, I sat on the couch so full that I could hardly move. I'd eaten too much. But the food had been delicious, and constantly putting another bite of it into my mouth had saved me from having to make too much conversation with any of the people I didn't know.

But one of those people, Tony Kramer, had followed me into the living room and had helped himself to the chair nearest me. "Hey," he said.

Somehow I had expected something more profound. He'd followed me, after all. I smiled. "Hey."

He tapped the arm of his chair a few times. "I've seen you at church . . ."

I folded my hands in my lap. "I've seen you there too."

"I'm sorry I haven't talked to you before now."

"That's okay," I said. "Why should you have talked to me before now?"

"Well, because you're new here."

I considered that and then smiled. "Are you the official welcoming committee? Because, if you are, I'll have to talk to Uncle Ben about finding—"

"No," he said. "It's nothing like that."

"I know. It—it was a joke."

He nodded. "I know. I mean, I knew that."

"Good," I said.

And then we sat there. Looking at, and then away from, one another. I wondered why he didn't just get up and leave. Or why I didn't. I was curious, I supposed, because I couldn't help feeling that he'd had something specific in mind to say to me, and he hadn't yet said it.

I decided to put out a tester. "So, you're a senior this year?"

"Yeah."

"What do you plan to do when you graduate?"

"I'm not sure."

"Do you have any classes with Nathan?"

"I go to the other high school."

Silence again.

That line of questioning certainly hadn't accomplished anything! I took a moment to look closely at Tony Kramer while he looked down at his knees. Short dark hair. Dark eyes. A handsome enough face. He was wearing a rugby jersey—the real thing, it looked like. Some Australian team.

"That's a nice shirt," I ventured. "Christmas present?"

"No," he said. "I spent the summer in Australia on a student exchange program."

"Wow. You must be smart."

"I do all right," he said.

"So, it was winter when you were down there?"

"Yeah." He smiled. "But I was in Queensland, which is in the north, so it was nice."

"That's good."

More silence.

I'd done my part to get a conversation going, I figured. So I waited to see if he'd say anything. When he didn't, I stood up, stretched, and said, "I'm going to go see if Aunt Esther needs any help in the kitchen." I knew that she didn't. There were already so many people in there that they were probably in each other's way. But it was a good excuse to leave.

Tony's uneasiness had unnerved me.

"Wait." He stood, too, and stepped toward me. "I should have talked to you before now. You know, at church. But—"

"I already told you it's okay, Tony," I assured him. "Really."

"I guess the reason I didn't is, well, I didn't feel like I could just come up to you and say 'hi.' I mean, your parents are gone and . . ." He shoved his hands into his pockets. "A person should acknowledge that. But I didn't know what to say. I saw how you tensed up whenever people said stuff to you, and I didn't want to be just one more person adding to it."

It had not occurred to me that people would feel uncomfortable around me because of my parents' death. But now that Tony had mentioned it, I recalled how I had felt around my friend Beth when her father had been seriously injured in a farming accident. I hadn't known what to say, so for a while I had avoided her. Until we knew that her father was going to survive and almost fully recover.

"You're sweet, Tony," I said. "And I understand." I shrugged. Now it was my turn to be nervous! "There's really nothing anyone can say, anyway."

"I suppose not."

We walked together to the dining room and sat side by side at the table. We talked a little more about school, and Australia, and Montana, but after a while settled in with pie (Just what I needed . . . more food!) and listened to the adults.

Since most of the women had gone to the kitchen to deal with what had to be a continuously growing stack of dishes, the conversation at the table was decisively masculine. Hunting. Trucks. Politics. With each opportunity I got to observe my uncle with people, I appreciated more and more why he was so good at what he did. And today was no different. He knew how to direct a conversation. He knew how to follow one. And he knew when to do one or the other. He remembered details. His attention didn't wander. He didn't interrupt. But the thing that most impressed me was that even though he was the pastor of every man at the table, and this was his house, nobody seemed to feel the least bit unsettled.

Except Connor.

He was watching our uncle as well, his expression sour with misplaced contempt. Sour like the stench of a dirty wet sock carelessly tossed into a basket of clean clothes. I knew Connor. I knew how he tended to respond to hardship. With anger. Mom and Dad were dead—a definite and paralyzing hardship. So Connor was angry. Fine. Understandable. But why had he decided to attach that anger to Uncle Ben? Yes, Uncle Ben had decided that Connor and I would attend church with him each Sunday morning. Yes, he had certain expectations about what would and wouldn't be accepted in his home. But it seemed that Connor had been brooding at Uncle Ben ever since we'd arrived here. In fact, since before we'd arrived here. It didn't make any sense to me. And it wasn't fair.

But there was nothing I could do to change it. Or to convince my brother that he'd drawn his battle line in the wrong ground. I'd tried in the past; so had Mom and Dad, and it had always been a waste of time. Connor would disengage when he was good and ready, and not before.

Though I hoped that Connor would make that decision soon, I wasn't expecting him to. I had a sickening feeling that Uncle Ben would be fighting off headaches for a sizable chunk of the foreseeable future.

I looked to the other end of the table at my uncle as he laughed about something Stephanie's father had just said, and I determined that to whatever degree my brother was a grief to him, I would be a support. It would mean that I'd be setting myself against my brother, but I didn't care. Uncle Ben had been nothing but good to us, and Connor had been nothing but obnoxious in return.

As soon as I saw something I could do for Uncle Ben, I stood up to do it. And I made sure Connor noticed. I walked around the table, reached around Uncle Ben to grab his coffee cup, and said, "I'll get you some more."

"Thank you," he said.

To be polite, I asked the other men if any of them could use a refill, but my goal was to help my uncle and to annoy my brother in the process. I was pleased to see, in both of their faces, that I was succeeding.

But when I came back from the kitchen and was about to set the cup on the table, Nathan and Judah ran into the room behind me and one of them bumped me. Hot coffee spilled all over Aunt Esther's ivory lace tablecloth—and into Uncle Ben's lap.

He jumped up instantly. "Whew, I won't be needing any caffeine now, Brenna!"

"I'm sorry," I said. "I'm sorry."

"It's my fault, Dad." Nathan handed his father a towel. "I bumped into her."

"It's okay," he said.

But I could have cried, and probably would have if I hadn't happened to notice the satisfied half-grin on Connor's face. Then I was too angry to cry.

"Where were you going in such a hurry?" Uncle Ben asked Nathan as he finished wiping down his chair.

"We're going to go drive over the snow mounds in the parking lot at the church."

Uncle Ben stared up at his son with such a look of disbelief that nobody in the room could keep from laughing. Not me. Not even Connor. "You are kidding . . . right?"

"No," Judah confessed. "I got that new lift kit on and—"

Now even Uncle Ben was laughing. "Well, by all means!" He waved at his sons and started walking toward the stairs. "I'm going to go change. I'll be down in a second. Oh, and Judah?"

"Yeah, Dad?"

"Don't call me if you get stuck."

"Yes, sir." He looked at Connor. "Stephanie and Rebekah are coming with us, but we have room for one more. Do you want to come?"

"I'm sorry about the coffee," I called to Uncle Ben's back.

"Don't worry about it," he said to me. Then he turned to face the dining room again. "You should go, Connor. It'll be interesting, if nothing else."

I glanced at my brother. As kids, we'd often endured the boring walk to town just to slide on plastic bags down the plow hills at the corner of the "mall" parking lot. Now that I knew what a mall really was, I cringed that we'd ever called ours that. A long, skinny building with a fake log cabin front that housed every business in town. The post office, the bank, the café, the ranch supply store, the grocery store, and the gas station. That was it. Oh, and the bar. But the parking lot was large and situated perfectly to catch drifts, so Mr. Larsen in his tractor with the plow scoop on the front could usually scrape together some pretty decent snow mounds. Sledding down them had always been fun. I could only imagine how much more exciting it would be to drive over them in a beefed-up 4×4, even if it was a bit childish. Connor would be foolish not to go.

He looked at Judah for a moment, then at Uncle Ben, and then at me. "Yeah, well, I don't want to go."

"Suit yourself," Judah said. "Do you want to come, Brenna?"

I watched Uncle Ben turn and walk slowly up the stairs. "No, thanks," I told Judah. "I'm so full I'd probably burst at the first bump."

The truth was that I no longer wanted to do anything at that moment but lure my brother out of the room and away from everyone else so that I could give him a not-so-sweet piece of my mind. So when Judah, Nathan, Rebekah, Stephanie, and Tony Kramer—who jumped up to claim my seat as soon as I'd declined it—had gone, I sat in front of the piece of pie I had no intention of finishing and waited for an opportunity. But none came.

Chapter 7

I woke the next morning before the sun had fully brightened the cloudless sky. I lay in bed for a while, thinking, and then reached for the nightstand, for the picture Uncle Ben and Aunt Esther had given me for Christmas. It was an enlarged photo of Mom and Dad and Connor and me that had been taken the one time we'd gone to Alaska to visit. The day had been sunny. The mountains behind us were beautiful. All of us were smiling. It was a photo that had not been sent to Mom and Dad, so I'd never seen it. It was one of the only photos I had of all four of us together.

I'd cried when I'd opened it. And again when Aunt Esther had told me that the sturdy wood frame they'd put it in had been given to them by my father when they'd gotten married. Dad had made it and had carved a rose in the bottom right corner.

"I can't take it from you," I'd said.

"We want you to have it," Uncle Ben had assured me.

It was a treasure. No question. I held it close to me for a moment before setting it back on the nightstand and getting quietly out of bed. Rachel was still asleep on an air mattress on the floor, and I didn't want to wake her.

I pulled on my robe—Mom's robe—and walked out of the room.

The house was silent, so I was surprised to see light coming from the kitchen when I got to the bottom of the stairs.

It was Judah. Fully dressed. Sitting at the table with a bowl of cereal that looked to have gone soggy long ago in front of him.

I poured myself a glass of milk. "You're up early."

He shrugged. "So are you."

"Yeah, but I'm still in my pajamas." I pulled out a chair and sat down. "The idea is to eat that stuff before it absorbs all the milk."

He glanced down at his breakfast as if he was surprised to see it there.

"Are you all right?" I asked him. "You look, oh, I don't know, distracted."

"I'm all right," he said. "And believe me, I'm plenty focused."

I grinned. "About what happened at the snow mound yesterday?"

He'd burned up his clutch trying to get his outfit unstuck from one particular hill that had not packed down and hardened enough to support a vehicle. His Jeep had sunk right in. To the axles. But, hey, he'd just put on that new lift kit, right? And if he could just crank up the old horsepower while he centimetered forward and back a few thousand times . . .

He laughed. "No. That's not a good thing. But it's fixable."

"Expensive," I said.

"You know it."

"Your dad wasn't too happy about having to go get you," I said.

"I know. But I don't think he was surprised."

"If he thought you were going to have trouble," I said, "why didn't he suggest that you find something else to do?"

Judah smiled. "He did in his own way when he told me not to call him if I got stuck. But he has this philosophy about non-life-threatening-experience-learned-lessons. He figures they have a more lasting impact than him telling us why we shouldn't do whatever it is we want to do."

"I see." I smiled. "And is he right?"

"They're pretty convincing."

I laughed.

My cousin Judah and I had never been particularly close. We were three years apart, which didn't seem like much at our current ages, but the gap had put us in completely different categories as children. The difference between 12-almost-13 and just-turned-16, the ages we'd been the last time we'd seen one another, hadn't seemed quite so wide. But that had been right after that boy in Alaska had drowned, and Judah, understandably, had come to Montana without his usual enthusiasm. He'd been quiet, and unsure, and seemed to need to be near Uncle Ben at all times.

"They were horrible to him, Dee," Aunt Esther had told my mother one morning when she thought they were alone on the porch. "Tommy's father, most of all. I can't see how he's going to come through this with any kind of—"

"He will," my mother had assured her. "He's got you and Ben. And his faith." She'd placed both of her hands firmly on Aunt Esther's shoulders. "And when he gets enough distance from this to wade through all the garbage, he'll understand that it wasn't his fault."

"I don't see how," Aunt Esther had said. "But I hope you're right."

I wondered now, as I looked across the table at my cousin, if Mom had been right. If Judah had come to terms with the circumstances of that boy's death. But I wasn't about to ask. He'd obviously dealt with it enough to move his life forward in a positive direction in spite of it. And maybe that was all one could expect or hope for.

"I'm going to fry up some eggs," I told him as I lifted his cereal bowl from the table and set it on the counter. "I'm hungry. And maybe you'd actually eat your breakfast if it smelled good."

He smiled up at me. "Maybe so. Thanks."

"Well, I have a very fragile ego," I teased. "If there's any left on your plate, I'll think it's because they tasted bad and I'll never fry eggs again."

"You really should deal with that little issue, Brenna. A fragile ego can be debilitating. I just happen to know an excellent counselor who—"

I laughed. "Be quiet."

He did.

I fried the eggs, put some on a plate for each of us, grabbed silverware and two napkins, and set it all on the table. Judah asked a blessing on the food and thanked me for making it.

Then we started eating. I did, at least.

"Judah," I said, "step number one would be picking up your fork."

"Right. Sorry." He picked it up, made a couple of attempts at getting some food on it, and then set it back down. "I guess you know we're getting more company today?"

"Your friends from Alaska." I nodded.

"Yeah." He looked straight at me. "Tommy Cook's parents and sister."

Suddenly the eggs in my mouth tasted like a brown paper bag. I had to force myself to swallow them.

What had Aunt Esther said about Judah and stress? No wonder he wasn't eating. "Wow, Judah," I said. "I thought they hated you, you know, because they thought it was your fault—"

"They did," he said. "But Ashton—that's his sister—and I ended up on the same mission team last summer and we . . . I don't know. I guess we sort of came to an understanding about it and—"

"And now they're visiting you for Christmas." I shook my head. "Now I know why you all haven't been jumping for joy about seeing your company from Alaska."

"Their coming is a good thing," Judah insisted. "It really is. If Dad and Mr. Cook can make a start on restoring their friendship, if any of us can, then it's worth it. I know that's what God would want. It's just that it's kind of scary." He grabbed his fork and started tapping it against his plate. I suspected that he wasn't even aware that he was doing it. "Especially thinking about being face to face with Tommy's dad."

No longer interested in food, I took my plate and Judah's to the sink. When I came back to the table, I sat in the chair closest to him. "Judah, you said you and Tommy's sister came to an understanding?"

He nodded.

"You don't still think it's your fault, do you? The drowning?"

"No," he said. Right away, but not too quickly.

He was telling the truth.

"And," he said, "according to Ashton, they don't either. But there's still a lot of stuff between us. Stuff that was said. Stuff that happened."

All I could think to say was, "I'm sorry, Judah. This has got to be really tough."

"God has pieced a lot of things together to give our two families this opportunity to have real healing," he said. "Healing of the situation as well as the individual people in it. I mean, I could be at peace about it here, and Mr. Cook could be at peace about it there in Alaska, but it's so like God to want us to be at peace about it together besides." He smiled and shook his head. "That didn't make any sense."

"Yes it did," I said. "But, like you said, when you're face to face with Mr. Cook, your mind is sure to flash on all the hateful things he said to you, and—"

"Exactly. And I want to handle it right. The way God would want me to."

"Most people would be content if they could get through the meeting without anyone winding up unconscious on the living-room floor from a fist in the face," I said. "Seriously."

"Maybe," he said. "But why settle for being content with getting through when you can have the win?"

It was statements like that that made me realize just how down to the dirt real-life Christianity could be when a person chose to truly live it. It didn't have to be limited to someone's philosophy, or religion, or way of thinking about things. It could be real-life. And life changing.

But could it work in this situation?

This afternoon, when Uncle Ben, or Nathan, or whoever, pulled open the front door of their home to welcome Tommy Cook's sister, mother, and father, would any of them be able to think beyond the last words they'd exchanged, the things they'd all lost, Tommy's dead body stuck beneath a root at the bank of the river?

I had to wonder.

Chapter 8

"You've grown."

From my spot beside Connor on the couch, I could see everyone. Uncle Ben, Aunt Esther, Judah, Nathan, Rachel . . . Mr. and Mrs. Cook, and Ashton. It looked like some kind of bizarre face-off. Ewen vs. Cook. They had exchanged pleasantries when the Cooks had first arrived and had been welcomed in by Uncle Ben. Good flights? Yes. Did you have good connections? Yes. You're looking well. As are you. Then the standing there had started. Mrs. Cook still clutching her purse. Nathan still holding the pocket computer game he'd been distracting himself with all afternoon. Ashton looking around the room, taking in the sight of Aunt Esther's things as if she was cataloging them, making sure nothing was missing.

And then Mr. Cook had spoken.

And now Judah was nodding in reply. "Yes, sir."

I watched Mr. Cook closely. He was huge. Tall. Standing stiff and straight, like one of those mirthless-looking British palace guards. "You've changed your hair," he said to Judah. "It used to be fuller up on top."

"Yes, sir," Judah said again. Then he shoved his hands in his pockets. "Yours did too, sir."

Slowly, a smile found its way to Mr. Cook's lips. "True enough," he said. Then he held out his hand.

Without hesitation, Judah clasped it.

And then it was as if some invisible director had called out "Action!" Rachel offered to take Mrs. Cook's bag and coat. Ashton stepped forward to pull Aunt Esther close in what was obviously a long-awaited embrace. Mr. Cook nodded at Uncle Ben. It wasn't episode one of All Is Right in This Here World. Nathan wouldn't look anyone in the eye, and Uncle Ben seemed to be cautious over Judah as the two of them spoke with Mr. Cook.

But it was better than what I had expected.

Impressively better.

"This is amazing," I whispered to Connor.

"It's stupid," he whispered back. "Nathan told me some of the things that guy said to Judah." He folded his arms across his chest and shook his head. "He wouldn't be welcome in my house."

"You're right," I said sarcastically. "We wouldn't want to be happy, or move on, or anything. It's much more fun to stay mad."

"Brenna, you don't understand." Even in his whisper I could hear tired frustration replacing his initial anger. "It's not that cut-and-dried."

"I never said it was cut-and-dried. Actually, I think the word I used was 'amazing.' " I thought of the song. "Amazing Grace." Forgiveness. From God to sinner. From sinner to sinner. Amazing each and every time.

The Cooks stayed for nearly two hours. Plans were agreed upon for the following day, and then, saying that they were tired from their trip, they left to get back to their hotel. It took several minutes after the door had been shut behind them for someone to begin moving into the normal routine of evening. It was Judah, who said, "I guess this is as good a time as any to tear into that transmission."

"I'll help you," Connor said.

I watched them dig through the front closet for two coveralls as Aunt Esther and Rachel headed to the kitchen to get started on dinner, and Uncle Ben went to the den to finish putting together his sermon for the midweek service. Nathan figured that the driveway could probably use another shoveling and went outside to see to it.

Judah and Connor left me alone in the living room after they'd found the coveralls and two pairs of sturdy work gloves. I was a little surprised by, but glad about, Connor's offer to help Judah. My brother loved to work on cars, and he'd had plenty of practice. It seemed that something was always in need of repair at Grandpa's ranch—and who wanted to pay a mechanic when you could do it yourself and generate some healthy male bonding in the process? I didn't think that Connor had ever dropped a transmission, though, so this was an opportunity for an as-yet-to-be-conquered challenge. And Judah could definitely use the help. Those things had to weigh several hundred pounds. Even with the transmission jack they had managed to rent that morning, it would be a two-man job.

I grabbed the throw from the back of the couch, unfolded it over myself, and shut my eyes. When I opened them again, the house was dark except for the lamp on the table at the bottom of the stairs, and silent. When I moved to push the throw aside, I realized that someone had put a second one over it. I stood up, stretched, folded both throws, and walked stiffly toward the kitchen for a glass of water.

I could see the garage window through the window at the kitchen sink, and the light was still on out there. I put on one of the coats hanging near the back door—Uncle Ben's, I supposed—and trudged through the snow toward the cracked open side door. "Hey," I called out, so that I wouldn't startle anyone and make him smack his head on hard metal. "It's getting pretty late. How's it going?" All I could see was someone's legs sticking out from underneath the outfit. They'd lifted it up on four wood blocks, and the transmission, transfer case, flywheel, etc. had been lowered to an accessible position underneath.

"It's dropped, anyway," Judah said. He slid out and got to his feet. "I was just picking up the tools."

"Where's Connor?"

"He went in when Dad came out."

Even though I felt a sudden spark of anger at my brother, amusement overpowered it. So Uncle Ben hadn't completely abandoned Judah to the consequences of his own stupidity after all. I smiled. "Your dad helped you, huh?"

"Yeah," Judah said. "Don't sound so surprised." He tossed a ratchet into the tool chest, shut the lid, and shoved it back on the bench until it thudded against the wall. Then he went to the sink at the corner, and the smell of cold metal and grease was momentarily smothered by the smell of citrus as he scrubbed his hands. He pulled off his coverall, turned off the garage light, pulled the door shut, and walked back to the house with me.

Once we were inside, I offered to put on some water for hot chocolate. The garage was heated but not warm, and working or not, Judah had to be cold.

"Thanks," he said. "Sounds good."

When the water was on the stove to boil, I went to the refrigerator and dug around inside. "Did your mom put up any leftovers?" I asked him.

"I don't know," he said. "I didn't come in for dinner."

"Well, are you hungry?"

"You know what? I am."

Of course he was. He hadn't eaten anything all day. "I'll fix us something," I said. "I slept through dinner, so I'm hungry too."

"I'll help you."

We decided to make one sub-style sandwich on a loaf of French bread and split it. While I piled on the condiments, coldcuts, and cheese, he sliced tomatoes and black olives and put them on.

"You better cut my half in half," I told him. "I'll never be able to eat all that."

He did it, and then we took our plates to the table. After he'd asked the blessing, and we'd started eating, he looked steadily at me and said, "My dad's a good person, Brenna."

I swallowed the bite I'd just taken whole. "I know that."

Why would he say that to me?

As if the question had shown in my expression, he said, "It seems like you and Connor, especially Connor, don't like him very much. I mean, why would it surprise you that he'd help me?"

"It was a joke more than anything, Judah," I said.

"So it didn't surprise you?"

I shrugged. "Maybe a little, but—"

"He's my dad. It's a big job. Why wouldn't he help me?"

I grinned. "Because it happened when you were being stupid."

"I wasn't being stupid." He smiled. "Okay, I wasn't being smart. But . . . so?"

"So I thought that Uncle Ben would, you know, let you suffer everything there was to suffer and hopefully learn your lesson because of it."

Judah thought about that. "Is that what your dad would have done?"

"No," I said instantly.

"Why should my dad be so different?"

"He does have a reputation," I said, "with Grandma and Grandpa, anyway, of being too strict with you guys sometimes."

"But it goes way beyond that with Connor," Judah said.

I nodded. It did. There was no use trying to cover for my brother, or pretending to be startled by Judah's observation—as if it was without merit. Connor's attitude was obvious to everyone.

"What's his problem?"

"I don't know," I said.

"I can't figure it out, either," he said. "And he was definitely not open to clueing me in."

"You asked him?"

"In roundabout ways." He shook his head. "No go, though."

I stared down at a tomato slice that was about to slip out of my sandwich. "He probably doesn't even know."

"If that's true," Judah said, "and he's not mad at Dad but just mad, he needs to give it up, or find somewhere else to put it, or something, because I can tell you that all my dad wants to do is be there for Connor. And you." He stood and took his empty plate to the sink to rinse it off. When he'd finished, he looked back at me. "And he'll prove it too. Whatever it takes."

When I went to the sink a second or two later with my plate, Judah, who was still standing there, said, "Brenna, can I ask you something and have you not tell anyone that I'd asked you?"

I shrugged. "Sure."

"If you were going to get an engagement ring, would you rather pick it out yourself, or have the guy who's proposing to you pick it out and surprise you?"

"Hmmm." I grinned at him. "Now, why would you be asking me something like that, I wonder."

His face flushed a little and he smiled. "Just answer the question."

"I guess it would depend on the guy proposing," I said. "If he had decent enough taste to pick out a ring I'd want to wear for the rest of my life, then the surprise could be very romantic."

"What if the guy proposing could get help, say, from an older sister in choosing an appropriate ring?"

I balanced the benefits of both scenarios and made my decision. It took all of three seconds. "I'd want him to surprise me."

Chapter 9

The next day, while Uncle Ben, Judah, and Mr. Cook were out in the garage hoping to successfully replace the clutch and reattach the transmission without any stripped bolts or bloodied knuckles, Rachel, Ashton, and I decided to give Rebekah a call. Aunt Esther and Mrs. Cook were sitting at the kitchen table for a long overdue conversation, and Nathan and Stephanie had borrowed her father's snowmobiles to take Connor to the mountains to show him the trails.

"I don't care what we do," Ashton said. "I just want to see her while we're here."

Ashton had met Rebekah during the mission trip that Judah had told me about. They hadn't become instant friends, for obvious reasons, but Ashton now assigned Rebekah the credit, almost entirely, for opening her heart to finding peace inside herself about her brother's death, and then, as an extension of that, making peace with Judah.

The more I learned about everyone involved in the situation—the things they had been through and were now resolving—the more I admired them. Their strength, which they all attributed to God, was making me wonder about my own understanding of His role in my life. I knew that I believed in Him, was trusting Him to save me, and would say that I loved Him to anyone asking if I did . . . but that had always been about as far as it had gone. He was God, way up there somewhere, too big and holy to be bothering about the small details of my life. I knew the Ten Commandments and the basic rules of the Christian religion and followed them without an alarming number of exceptions. But did I believe that He could move and enable me to do something that would grate as noisily against my nature as forgiving someone who'd falsely accused me of being the cause of someone's death? Or forgiving someone who, for a time at least, I'd blamed for the death of someone I loved? Or acknowledging my error in either of these circumstances, not only to myself and God, but to the people my error had most hurt?

I did not know that I did.

And what about the acceptance of someone's death as part of God's sovereignty? Ashton claimed to have found peace in Tommy's death as part of some sort of huge puzzle God was putting together. And, hadn't Uncle Ben said basically the same thing when he'd asked me if it really mattered whether five and five made ten, or three and three and four, as long as I had confidence in the mathematician who'd worked the equation to come up with the right answer?

Maybe I didn't really trust the "mathematician" as much as I would say I did to someone asking.

"How about bowling?" Rachel was asking me. "The four of us. I don't think I'm up for anything outside today. It's cold."

"Sure," I answered. "I like bowling."

The truth was that I was terrible at bowling, but Rachel, Rebekah, and Ashton turned out to be equally unskilled, so it didn't matter. After only two games, more than half of which had been spent waiting for the ball to make its way to the end of the gutter, we decided to soften the humiliation of such a pathetic-but-humorous showing—with food.

Rebekah chose the place. A small, family-owned Chinese buffet.

"So," she asked after we'd all served ourselves and Ashton had asked the blessing, "how did it go yesterday?"

Ashton took a sip of hot tea. "It was tense at first," she said. "But everyone settled down, and it went fine."

"Judah didn't call me," Rebekah said, "so I was a little worried."

"He was working out in the garage until really late," I told her.

She smiled down at the chunk of sweet-and-sour pork she'd just put on her fork. "Sometimes he handles things with so much maturity that it amazes me," she said. "And then sometimes, he's like a six-foot-tall ten year old!"

Rachel nodded her agreement. "But you love him anyway."

"Yes I do."

I tried to hide a smile of my own behind my egg roll as I glanced carefully at Rachel. Had Judah already talked with her, the way he'd talked with me, about his engagement ring for Rebekah? Seeing nothing revealing in her expression, I looked back at Rebekah. Did she know or suspect that Judah had begun to not only think but also plot in the direction of asking her to marry him?

Judging by everything I'd been told by people who knew Judah and Rebekah, the eventuality of him proposing and her accepting was not in question. It was *when?* that had people talking. I'd heard plenty of it and had even been asked about it a couple of times—as if I would know! Would Judah wait until he'd finished school—three-and-a-half more years? Would he decide that that was way too long a postponement of the inevitable and ask her tomorrow? Or would he settle on some as yet to be determined date in between?

Rebekah's face was as empty of clues as Rachel's. It looked as if I'd have to wait along with everyone else for my cousin to act.

I leaned back in my chair and listened as I ate while Rebekah and Ashton brought each other up-to-date on all the things that had happened in their lives since the mission trip. They spoke a lot about Judah, quite a bit about someone named Shane, and briefly about several other things.

When their conversation had trickled down to several seconds of pause, Ashton turned her attention to me. She watched me the whole time she was finishing her meal, and finally she set her fork and napkin on her plate. "How are you doing, Brenna?" she asked me quietly.

The concern in both her tone of voice and in her eyes convinced me that she wasn't asking me if I was enjoying my food or their company. "Okay, I guess," I told her.

"How long has it been now?"

"Eight weeks tomorrow," I said.

She shook her head. "I remember being nothing but numb for so long after Tommy died. Months."

I laughed a little. "I don't think I'm numb. I cry all the time. My brother gets irritated with me."

"Crying is good," Ashton said. "Don't be ashamed of it."

"I'm not. I wonder when it'll stop, is all."

She nodded. "Take it from me," she said, "be sad when you're sad. It's when you try to shove it away, or onto something else, that you really harm yourself. Sad is a whole lot easier to heal up from than bitter—or numb."

I didn't doubt that she knew what she was talking about. And I appreciated her courage in approaching the subject with me. I did. I just didn't want to talk about this anymore. I didn't want to end up crying again. Not in a restaurant. Not when our day together had been so enjoyable so far. "I'll do it," I said.

And then I realized that in saying "I'll do it" I'd done just the opposite!

"What if I'm sad right here?" I asked Ashton. "Right now?"

"Then we're here for you," Rachel promised me.

"Brenna, you're still counting in weeks," Ashton said. "Your loss is unimaginable. Even to me. Of course you're going to be sad right here and right now. Anyone who tries to tell you that you shouldn't be is an idiot."

Even as tears filled my eyes, I couldn't help laughing. "Then I'm an idiot, and so's Connor!"

Slowly, and with effort that was humorous to watch, Ashton dismissed her initial astonishment at my reaction to what she'd said and started to laugh too. Eventually, Rachel joined her so that the three of us were laughing and crying and making absolute idiots of ourselves in public. Which only made us laugh and cry more.

So did Rebekah's you-guys-have-been-under-way-too-much-stress expression as she watched us and circled the tip of her spoon along the rim of the little blue and white bowl of hot mustard. But then the server came by to refill our water glasses, and suddenly, nothing was funny. I swallowed back the air that had caught in my throat and wiped at my eyes with my napkin.

"Sorry," I said to Rebekah when the server had gone.

She shrugged. "You know what they say about laughter."

I nodded. I knew. And I did feel better for having allowed myself to laugh. It was what I had laughed about that worried me. But not too much.

We left the restaurant as quickly and quietly as we could after that and drove straight back to the house. The men had come in from the garage and were sitting in front of a fire in the fireplace, warming up for a few minutes before rushing off in separate directions to get ready for dinner and the evening service at the church. Rebekah found a spot to sit beside Judah, and Ashton squeezed in next to her father and made the necessary introductions. Since Rachel had gone to the kitchen to see if her mother needed any help with anything, I sat down next to Uncle Ben.

"Are Nathan and Connor back yet?" I asked him.

"No," he said. "They're going to meet us at church."

I shuddered, and then dismissed it. Connor wouldn't complain about attending midweek service—it was a small price to pay for a whole day of fun. Besides, he was with Nathan, not Uncle Ben, and Nathan had no obligation to be patient, loving, or mindful of walls being built or torn down. No serious obligation, anyway. And this was Nathan. He would just tell Connor to put a sock in it.

"Do you like snowmobiling, Brenna?" Judah asked me.

"Yeah," I said. "I've only done it on the plains, though. You know how it is around the ranch. I bet it's really fun up in the mountains."

Uncle Ben put his arm around my shoulders and pulled me close to him. "I'll have to take you up there sometime."

"I'd like that," I said. I leaned against my uncle and tried to pretend that his strong arm around me didn't remind me of the times I'd snuggled in near to my father. Then I decided not to pretend, but to remember. And amazingly, I didn't cry.

Chapter 10

By Sunday morning, New Year's Eve day, the Cooks had gone home, Judah's 4×4 was roadworthy again, and all the Christmas decorations—what few of them there were—had been packed up and put away. Rachel, Aunt Esther, and I had made a huge breakfast of eggs, bacon, hash-browns, and fruit, which everyone had enjoyed.

And now it was time to leave for church.

I'd been looking forward to going to church again since the midweek service. More specifically, I'd been looking forward to it since my conversation afterwards with Ashton about looking to God. Really looking to God. For peace. For insight. For purpose from here on out. While I'd paid attention to all of Uncle Ben's sermons that I'd heard so far, I hadn't absorbed them. My uncle was a competent public speaker. Engaging. Articulate. Passionate about and studied up on his subject matter. But the subject matter itself, even though it was God and therefore relevant to every human being, had thus far not penetrated my audience member mentality about going to church and hearing the preacher preach.

This morning, though, the subject matter was what I wanted to consider. For me. For my life now. For real.

Connor, however, was making it obnoxiously clear that he wasn't interested in the subject matter, or the presentation, or anything else. He did not want to go to church. And he wasn't going to go to church. He'd made the announcement, and he had sauntered over to the couch to sit and glare at Uncle Ben. "And you can't make me, either."

"Oh, Connor." I shook my head and leaned forward in Aunt Esther's rocking chair. "Don't do this."

But he was doing it. And he had everyone's attention.

Judah and Nathan stopped their conversation to stare first at Connor and then at Uncle Ben. Neither of them had ever tried such a thing, I was sure, and they were as curious as anyone else about what their father would do in response.

For several moments, Uncle Ben did nothing. Then, he went to the kitchen, made a phone call, and came back. He walked to the couch and scooped Connor up in a fireman's hold so quickly that Connor couldn't react until he was already upside-down over Uncle Ben's shoulder.

"Just so you know I can," Uncle Ben said. Then he set Connor on his feet, waited while he sat back down, and sat beside him. "You all go ahead," he said to Aunt Esther. "Rick's got a sermon he can pull out, and Connor and I need—"

"But—"

"Go ahead, Esther."

Uncle Ben's tone was firm enough, more firm than I'd ever heard it, and the words had been enunciated crisply enough that we all left the house without another protest, any questions, or even a good-bye.

"Oh, he's mad," Nathan whispered once we were outside.

"And with good reason," Aunt Esther countered, silencing even the thought of more discussion.

The assistant pastor, Rebekah's father, preached that morning, and he did a remarkably good job at it, too, considering he'd had all of eighteen minutes to prepare. But I found myself unable to really pay attention the way I had been intending to. Maybe it was because Uncle Ben wasn't preaching. Or maybe it was because I was too busy wondering what, exactly, Uncle Ben was doing at any given moment. At every given moment.

"Is your uncle sick today?" Tony Kramer asked me when the service had let out.

I was standing alone in the entryway waiting for Aunt Esther. She'd needed to get something from Uncle Ben's office. Judah, not surprisingly, had gone to the door with Rebekah and her father to shake people's hands as they left. Rachel was still in the sanctuary, talking to one of her friends who was also home for winter break. And Nathan, not any more surprisingly than Judah going with Rebekah, had offered to walk with Stephanie and her parents to their car.

"N-no," I told Tony, glad that he'd taken the initiative to come talk to me, but wishing that he hadn't asked me that particular question. "No. He's okay."

Although he might have a pretty good headache going by now, I thought.

"Hmm," Tony said. But he left it alone. "So how's it been going?"

"Okay."

"Are you nervous about starting school next week?"

I nodded. "Really nervous."

"Don't be," he said. "Your last name is Ewen."

I didn't understand. So what?

"The kids who gravitate toward you will probably be really nice to you, and the other kids, the ones who might have been into bugging the new kid, will probably stay away from you because they've already heard all they want to hear about Jesus."

"Are you saying my cousins are obnoxious about their faith?" I grinned.

"No. It's just part of who they are, and it comes out. That's all. At least that's what people have told me. I go to the other high school."

I remembered. "Well, Connor's there now too," I reminded him. "And he puts his own unique twist on Ewen."

He smiled. "I've kind of figured."

"He's just having a hard time dealing with . . . everything," I said. A little coldly. If I didn't defend my brother, who would? And it was true. He was having a hard time dealing with . . . everything. One moment he'd be proclaiming that he didn't believe in God, and the next, he'd be kicking the leg of his bed and yelling, "Why did You let any of this happen?" One day he'd spend the whole afternoon helping Aunt Esther with one of her projects around the house, and the next, he'd be in Rachel's room half the evening telling me how much he hated the place. The only constant in his behavior seemed to be his uncaring attitude toward Uncle Ben. "I don't think he knows for sure what he's feeling yet," I told Tony, "let alone how to deal with it."

Tony's expression softened instantly. "I don't know how either of you can deal with it. Honest."

I reached out and lightly touched the sleeve of his khaki dress shirt. "You're sweet, Tony," I said. And then I snapped my mouth shut and pulled my hand back. I had already said that to him once. Once was one time too many, and now I'd said it twice!

But he *was* sweet.

I could tell by his sudden interest in the binding of the Bible in his hands that my discomfort must be more obvious than I'd realized and that it was unnerving him. I struggled to think of something to say to put him at ease again.

But he thought of something first. "Speaking of Connor, where is he today?"

"He's home with Uncle Ben."

"Is he sick?"

I laughed. "No, Tony. He's not sick either."

Tony nodded like he thought he understood. And he probably did, though I doubted he was picturing anything even approaching the sight of his pastor hefting Connor over his shoulder like some oversized bag of salt.

"What?" he asked me. "Why are you smiling?"

"Trust me, Tony," I answered; "you really don't want to know."

"Well, it's a good sign you're smiling, anyway," he said. Then he smiled, too. It was a nice smile, I noticed. A sincere one. "Hey, I haven't seen you at youth group," he said. "Has Nathan told you about it?"

"Yeah. I guess I haven't felt like coming yet. Uncle Ben said the only service we have to attend is Sunday morning service."

"Oh." Tony stared at me as his fingers found the binding of his Bible again. "You don't want to be here?"

"You don't see me kicking and screaming, do you?" I thought about Connor and about what might have happened if Uncle Ben had decided to make him come this morning. I hoped that my brother possessed enough self-respect to get off Uncle Ben's shoulder and walk into the building on his own two feet. But, the way he'd been acting lately, kicking and screaming could very well have been his mode of entry. I tried not to, but I couldn't help smiling again.

Quickly, though, so Tony wouldn't ask me any more questions about what I was finding so funny, I said, "I have been thinking about starting at youth group. Can I consider your comment an official invitation? Will you meet me at the door and introduce me to everyone I haven't already met so I don't look like my cousin's tag-along?"

"Sure." Tony nodded, and his hand loosened up on his Bible. "I'd be happy to do that."

"Then I'll come this week."

We started walking together toward Aunt Esther, who'd just come out of the office and was pulling the door shut.

"Nathan probably wouldn't introduce you around, anyway," Tony said with a quiet tease in his voice. "At least not once Stephanie got there."

Even though I knew Tony wasn't being entirely serious, I defended my cousin. "Nathan's been really good about stuff like that," I said.

"Oh yeah?" He grinned. "So why were you standing alone this morning?"

I shrugged. What could I say? Except, "I am a big girl, Tony. It isn't like they have to worry about me running out into the parking lot and getting run—"

Just then, Nathan hurried past Judah and Rebekah at the door—I heard him asking them where I was. Then he ran up behind Tony and me. "Sorry, Brenna," he said, a little breathless.

Tony glanced at me. I shrugged again. And then we both started laughing.

Nathan was asking us, "What? What's so funny?" for the second time when Aunt Esther met up with us and said, "We're going straight home. Find Rachel and Judah and get your things."

"Yes, ma'am," Nathan said.

I could tell by his startled expression that he hadn't heard that tone of voice from his mother in years, and that "Yes, ma'am" had come out of his mouth automatically, as if he were a six-year-old child being told for the last time of what he knew would be only one last time to get to bed.

My aunt had had two hours to sit and consider the disrespect my brother had shown her husband, and her feelings about it obviously had not softened much. Her eyes did, though. "I'm sorry," she said quietly to Nathan. "Please go find your brother and sister and get your things."

"You got it," he said.

Tony squeezed my arm as he mouthed, "See you later." Then he nodded at Aunt Esther and hurried away from us back toward the entryway.

I stepped right up beside Aunt Esther as we followed him, hoping she'd recognize my support in the gesture.

She seemed to, but she still felt the need to apologize. She didn't want to make me feel uncomfortable, she said. Or like she expected me to choose sides. She understood that Connor is my brother.

"Yeah," I said. "And my brother is being a jerk."

At that, she smiled. A little.

"Aunt Esther?"

"Yes?"

"What do you think he and Uncle Ben have been doing all this time?"

"Honestly?" She shook her head. "I have no idea." She took her coat from Judah, slipped into it, and then accepted his arm for the walk across the icy parking lot.

Chapter 11

Neither Uncle Ben nor Connor was in the front room when I walked in behind Aunt Esther. I hung my coat in the closet and ran quietly up the stairs to see if Connor was in his room. Judah's room.

He was.

"What happened?" I hoped that the curiosity in my voice didn't overpower the concern. Both were present, especially now that I was with him. "Connor?" He was lying on the bed with his back to me. I wasn't even sure he was awake. But then he rolled onto his other side, sat up on the edge of the bed, and patted it to let me know I could sit down if I wanted to.

I did.

"He said I make him feel like he did when he was a kid," he said. "Frustrated. Like he used to get frustrated with Dad. He said I remind him a lot of Dad."

"Well you look exactly like him," I said.

"I know, I know. Except I have paler eyes. I know."

I smiled, remembering, as he no doubt was, what Mom had always said about his eyes. The color of the cookie part of the cookie, instead of the color of the chocolate chips, like your father's.

"That's not what Uncle Ben was talking about." He sounded tired.

I waited. He would continue when he was ready. When he'd chosen the right words. As I waited, I looked around the room. Judah hadn't done much with it as far as decorating, I observed. Of course, he was a boy. He probably didn't care about color schemes and matching accessories and a common theme to tie it all together—as Rachel had with all her red, black, and white. There was a five-shelf bookcase, which was full from top to bottom, in some places crammed so that I wondered if anyone would ever be able to remove a book. I skimmed the titles and came to the conclusion that nobody but Judah would want to anyway. Connor definitely wouldn't. There were a couple of award certificates hanging on the wall. A framed and autographed picture of a tennis player getting ready to swing at the ball. Jeremy somebody. I couldn't make out the last name. A photo album. An old baseball cap. And that was about it. I supposed that Judah could have taken things with him when he'd left for school, but I doubted it. The things that were here were obviously significant to him, and they were still here. No. He just must not be the type to gather or tolerate clutter, I decided.

Connor, however, had the whole closet full of clutter. Overflowing, in fact. True, he was living in somebody else's room and couldn't really make himself at home, even though Judah and everyone else had told him to. And true, we were still getting boxes from Grandpa and having to figure out what to do with more and more of our stuff. But Connor's room would never have won any tidiness awards, even at home. He might clean it up a bit more after Judah took the rest of his things out, but I wasn't planning to hold my breath.

"He says I'm not dealing with what's really bugging me," Connor said at last. "And that Dad used to do that."

"Dad did used to do that," I said, more to myself than to Connor. Now that it had been mentioned, put into words, I could see it plainly, and seeing it put my father into a whole new focus. One of those things I'd never understood about his temper suddenly made sense. Almost. "Remember, Connor? He'd get all upset about the hose still lying on the front lawn—how it was going to rob the grass of water and sunlight, and all that, not to mention flatten it. He'd go on and on about the grass, but really he was mad because you or I or Mom or whoever hadn't bothered to put the hose away. And he'd never just say 'You should have put the hose away.' It was the grass this, and the grass that, and then he'd go put the hose away."

Connor nodded. He remembered. "That's not what I'm doing, though," he said. "I know exactly what's bugging me, and I'm dealing with it."

"Connor—"

"What? Are you going to start on me too, Brenna? You don't think I've heard enough already this morning?"

I sighed and shook my head. "No. I'm not going to start on you."

"Good. Because you know what? I don't want to hear it." He stood up, walked to the closet, turned, and came back to the bed. He did it again. Twice. And then, finally, he sat back down on the edge of the bed to glare right in my face. "I don't care what he thinks, anyway. You know why? Because sooner or later he's going to let me down just like . . . and I'm . . . I'm not going to give him the chance. That's what's bugging me, and that's how I'm dealing with it."

Uncle Ben was going to let him down? What did he mean? Just like who? God, maybe? What was he talking about? "Connor, I—"

"Just leave me alone, Brenna."

Something in the emotion in his eyes made me nod in surrender. I'd back off. For now. "Is that all he said to you?"

He let out a scornful laugh as he shook his head. "I wish. That was only the beginning. Then there was the 'I know this is a difficult time for you, Connor; it's a change for all of us' lecture. And then the 'You're part of this family now' lecture." He laughed again. "Yeah. Whatever. And then, oh, and this is the kicker! Okay, and then he says, 'I'm not willing to pull back on this,

Connor. You don't have to like it. You don't have to agree with it. And you don't have to pretend to when you get there. But you will come to church.' Why do I have to go to church if I don't like it, or agree with it, or even believe it?" My brother looked at me as if I'd never be able to come up with an answer. "Huh?"

I gave him the first answer that came to mind. It came immediately. "Because you're fourteen years old and he's responsible for you."

"So he has to drag me to church?"

"He has to know where you are."

"Oh, come on." Connor was indignant. "Like I'm going to sit in his living room and commit some crime while he's out preaching! Give me a break!"

I stood up. It was past time to get out of this conversation. "Give him a reason to believe that that's not a possibility." I started toward the door and then turned back. "He doesn't know you, Connor, remember? Except maybe Dad told him about the time you spray painted that little profanity on Mr. Herschel's garage because he got after you to stay off his property—which is his right, by the way. Maybe Dad called and asked Uncle Ben for advice one of the sixty thousand times you stormed out of the house mad." I stopped to take a breath and leaned toward him just a little while I was at it. "And even if Dad never said a word to Uncle Ben about you, he's certainly putting together his own opinion. And right now he's got, let's see, some bad attitude, and more bad attitude, and, you guessed it, even more bad attitude to build that opinion with." I straightened up and shook my head. "Give him a break."

"Whose side are you on, anyway?" Connor shouted at me. He sounded ready to cry.

"I don't even see why there have to be sides, Connor." I sat beside him and shut my eyes. "Don't you get it?"

"You're just afraid to stand up to him."

"No. I'm not." Then I thought about how it would feel to be carried into church over Uncle Ben's shoulder and dropped onto my seat like a squirming, rebellious preschooler upset about her graduation from the nursery to The Pew—or in the case of Uncle Ben's church, The Folding Metal Chair. I had to smile. "Okay. Maybe a little. But—"

"But nothing."

"But it's not like he's being unreasonable," I finished. Then I softened my tone. It took a deliberate effort. "He's asking you to do something that lasts two, maybe three hours once a week. He's doing a whole lot more than that for us." I paused to let him absorb that. "Think about it."

But Connor didn't want to think about it. "I didn't want to come here," he said right away. "And neither did you."

"It was what Mom and Dad wanted," I reminded him.

"Yeah, well, they're dead."

That was it. I'd heard enough. I stood up and left the room without saying another word. And I made sure I slammed the door.

I went to my room across the hall to hide until I'd calmed down, but Rachel was in there, loading books into a cardboard box. I didn't feel like talking just then, so I muttered something about helping Aunt Esther with lunch and ran down the stairs with my head down, not sure where I thought I was going. By the time I'd reached the landing, I was so angry and upset and frustrated and confused—*Yeah, well, they're dead*—that I'd started to cry.

By the time I stepped off the bottom step, I was shaking.

How could Connor say that? Was he planning to live on like Mom and Dad had never existed, like what they'd wanted for us didn't matter, because they were gone now? Didn't he care that they had cared enough about what would happen to us if something ever happened to them that they had taken the time to

legally specify their wishes? Didn't he realize how those words—
they're dead—still stabbed at me? Didn't they stab at him?

What was wrong with him, anyway?

"Brenna? Are you all right?"

I'd been looking down, and my eyes were squinted shut
against tears. I'd run right into Uncle Ben. I didn't look up. I
didn't step back. I didn't open my eyes. I just stood there and
shook my head no.

He pulled me close and let me cry.

I could feel the cool silk of his tie against my flushed cheek.
I could taste the salt of my tears. I could hear his heart beating.

Yeah, well, they're dead.

I remembered what Ashton had told me and cried until I was
finished. Then, slowly, I stepped away from my uncle and wiped
at my eyes with the heels of my hands. "I'm sorry," I said to him.
"About your tie."

He held it up, pressed at the wet spot that would undoubtedly
dry discolored and misshapen, and then let it fall back against his
shirt. Then he shrugged. "It's ugly anyway."

I smiled at the smile in his eyes. And I meant it.

Connor didn't speak to me once the whole rest of the day, not
even when the bunch of us were sitting in front of the fireplace
and jokingly sharing our New Year's "Resolutions" at a little before midnight. And he didn't mention or apologize for our conversation at any time during the next week.

But on Sunday morning he was dressed for church and didn't
go anywhere near the couch. He wasn't happy about it, and he
made sure Uncle Ben understood that and felt it in no uncertain
terms, but he went. On his own two legs.

Score one for Big Sister.

Chapter 12

"Okay, let's have a look." Nathan held out his hand for my class schedule. We'd just stepped out of the main office and now stood in the hall. It was early, so there weren't a lot of students around yet, but I still felt nervous. Our entire school complex back home—grades K-12—would have fit into a fourth of this building. Canyon Street High was huge. And modern. Our footsteps on the shiny tiled floor echoed off the lockers that lined the walls.

"Big, huh?" Connor leaned toward me to whisper.

"Sure is."

"It's pretty easy to figure out, though," he said.

Nathan agreed. He showed me all around the building and pointed out the easiest ways to get from each of my classrooms to the next. By the time we finished our tour, several buses had pulled up in front, and the halls were filling with kids.

So many kids!

"Stephanie's waiting for us at the cafeteria," Nathan said. "We can get a cinnamon roll."

I'd already eaten breakfast, but I nodded and followed him.

"I'm out of here," Connor said. He hurried away from us and went back toward the main hallway.

Nathan watched him go. "He doesn't like my friends," he said. "It's kind of a tradition now for all the Christian kids at the school to meet together each morning over cinnamon rolls or whatever to talk and pray and stuff."

I nodded.

"There are some sophomores in the group," he said. "I'll introduce you if you want. Or you can skip it and head to your first class. It's up to you."

"No, I'll come. Thanks." I followed him to the cafeteria, expecting maybe a couple or three kids to be waiting for us there. But there were a lot more than that. Enough to fill three tables that seated eight, plus some standing around. "Wow," I whispered before I could stop to think better of it.

But Nathan didn't hear me. He was already saying hello to Stephanie and pulling me toward one of the sophomores he wanted to introduce me to.

I met his friends. I ate a cinnamon roll. I chatted with Stephanie and a few of the other girls. I started to relax.

And then one of the kids, Brian somebody, got our attention by banging his butter knife against the edge of his tray. "Okay," he said. "Anything anyone needs to pray about?"

A couple of kids mentioned a couple of things, and a couple more said they wanted prayer but wouldn't say why—an unspoken request, one of them called it. And then they prayed. Right there in the school cafeteria.

I knew it was rude, but I couldn't help it. I stared for a moment and then leaned toward Nathan and whispered, "Is this legal?"

"Yeah," he whispered back. "It's student led and run, so they can't touch us."

"But . . . right here in the cafeteria?"

He shrugged. "They wouldn't let us use a classroom." He smiled. "I guess they thought we'd back out of the idea of meeting and praying if we had to do it right out in the open and in front of our peers."

"That sure backfired on them, didn't it?" I muttered.

He nodded and smiled again, and I didn't miss his pleasure at the irony of it before he looked away from me to continue praying quietly.

Well, I had two choices. I could give in to my discomfort at the situation and get up and leave and alienate the kids in the school who would probably be the better friends to me. Or, I could forget about what the kids in the hallway were thinking as they giggled and strolled by, and I could bow my head and pray for the day.

I had to admit that I could use the prayer.

But it was an uncomfortable situation. I'd joined in at the prayer times in church, but only to the extent that I'd bowed my head, closed my eyes, and thought about God. I'd dreaded each and every night since coming to Colorado that Uncle Ben would ask me to bless the food. So far, he hadn't. I'd never prayed aloud. Not that I could remember. Except in first grade when I'd repeated the words of my Sunday school teacher when I'd asked Jesus to forgive my sins and be my Savior. But that was something different. I wasn't about to pray aloud, the way these kids were praying aloud, for the first time in the cafeteria of a public school.

On top of that, there were a couple of kids at the table, one in particular, who seemed to have no trouble praying aloud. Loudly aloud. I felt embarrassed for them and for myself because I was in the group with them. And then I felt ashamed for being embarrassed. I remembered the story of Daniel—at least, that's who I thought it was—who prayed three times a day right in front of his window where everyone could see him when he wasn't supposed to be praying to anyone but the king. He wasn't embarrassed.

Yeah, and he earned a trip to the lions' den, I reminded myself. Or was it the fiery furnace?

But Daniel—or maybe it was David—had survived, right? And hadn't the king turned to God after that?

Still, did this boy really have to say "Jesus" over and over again like he couldn't pull his teeth apart? I didn't think so. But I could ignore him. At least he was praying and not sitting around judging me—which was probably a good thing since I hadn't even said "Dear Lord" yet, silently or otherwise.

I bowed my head, closed my eyes, and . . . thought about God. That's all I knew how to do. I couldn't quite bring myself to address Him like He was Someone I could actually talk to. He was God! Something about saying, "Hi, God, it's Brenna. Could you please help it to go okay for me today? Thanks." It just didn't sit right with me. I wasn't sure why.

I'd heard Uncle Ben pray aloud, though, before and after his sermons and at the house. I'd heard Aunt Esther do it too. And Rachel, and Nathan, and Ashton. They all spoke to God the same way . . . respectfully, but conversationally. Like they really believed He was listening. One on one.

Could He be?

I wondered, and then I decided to ask Him. Silently.

Dear Lord, is it . . . is it okay if I talk to You like this?

There was no bolt of lightning striking me dead through the ceiling. Good. There was no angelic choir singing *Yes* to my soul. There was just a silent certainty inside that it was okay. So I ventured a little further.

Lord, I want You to be real to me. Like You're real to Uncle Ben.

I felt like I needed to clarify.

I mean, I know You are real. That you made everything and all that. I know that Jesus died on the cross for my salvation. I know there's a heaven and that Mom and Dad are there because they asked Jesus to forgive them. But sometimes, it's like You're so much bigger than me, and so far away from me, that You're not really real to me, even though You are real.

I shook my head and hoped that God understood what I was trying to say.

I had to grin. Of course He understood! He was God.

Anyway, I didn't want to overstep my bounds. Amen.

At about the same time, the kids in the cafeteria finished up their prayer time and I stood with Nathan to leave. He'd promised to walk me to my first class, and I intended to take him up on it. I couldn't remember which hallway I was supposed to turn into to get there.

"Okay, where are we going?" he asked me after we left Stephanie at her locker.

I dug my class schedule out of my pocket and unfolded it. "Room 217."

"That's this way," he said, and we headed up a flight of stairs.

As we walked, I debated whether or not to ask him how, exactly, God would answer my conversational prayer. Certainly not conversationally. But I decided against it. I didn't want Nathan thinking I was completely inept spiritually, even though I probably was. I'd have to stay alert, that's all, and hope I'd catch God's answer for myself.

The first half of the day went well. Smoothly. I found all my classes before the bell. Kids were generally nice to me. I liked all my teachers. I didn't get the impression that I was going to be behind or lost in any of my subjects.

Connor and I had the same lunch session, so we ate together. He'd made a couple of friends at school already, and he introduced me to them. My first impression was that their company wasn't going to be good for him, but I didn't say so. I tried not to stare at the one wearing the black T-shirt with white lettering that proclaimed "Satan is my neighbor's dog and he rules" . . . and wondered if anyone on the school staff had ever asked him not to wear that shirt in the classroom. Probably not.

The boy's name was Jimmy. He was friendly enough, and articulate, but he was a fourteen-year-old boy and it showed. He laughed at his own burps and thought it was hilarious when a girl accidentally dumped her tray and spilled macaroni and cheese and the juice from the fruit cocktail all over someone else's "way expensive" basketball shoes.

"So what do you think of Jimmy?" Connor wanted to know right after lunch. He'd left the cafeteria behind me and had chased me halfway to the stairs.

"I'm glad you're making friends," I told him. "I know you miss Kody."

"Nah." He shoved my comment back toward me with the back of his hand as if it had been something repulsive tossed at him that he could deflect. But I was not fooled. He did miss Kody. And his other friends back home. And Grandpa and Grandma.

"I'm going to see if Jimmy wants to come and hang out this weekend," he said. "You know, watch football, or something."

"At the house?"

"Yeah. At the house. Where else?"

I sighed and shook my head, but I couldn't deny a certain amount of amusement at the thought of my uncle's reaction to such a character. "You better tell him to wear a different shirt," I said.

"Hey." He shrugged. "I'm sure Uncle Ben is familiar with the First Amendment."

"Yeah," I said, "and he's also familiar with the location of his front door and how to direct someone through it and back outside."

I was joking, but Connor failed to find anything humorous about the suggestion. "He wouldn't kick my friend out of the house."

"No," I said seriously, choosing to surrender my point for the sake of peace. I didn't want to fight with him, or in any way fuel his arsenal of things to hurl at Uncle Ben. "He wouldn't."

"He'd probably want to, though, huh?" Connor was almost smiling, now, and I did not like the glee in his tone.

I grabbed his arm and turned him to face me. "Connor Ewen, you will not use Jimmy to get at Uncle Ben. That's not fair to anyone."

"Oh, what do you care?" He yanked his arm out of my hold and glared at me. "I saw the way you looked down your nose at him."

"I did not!"

"You did! The high and mighty little Christian girl looking down on the pathetic little whatever he is."

I laughed. I couldn't help it. "He's wearing a shirt that says Satan is his neighbor's dog, Connor. That's pretty weird."

Connor shook his head and looked at me as if I was the person to most be pitied in the situation. "It's just a shirt." And then he walked away.

I stood in the hallway, with kids passing by me on both sides going both ways, feeling trapped and unable to move. I did get myself moving, though, and hurried toward my locker.

Should I try to talk to Connor again? Or maybe I should skip that and go straight to Jimmy? Or Uncle Ben. It seemed to me that they had a right to know what Connor was up to. That they were about to become the components of an idiotic test.

But, what if I was wrong about my brother's intentions? I didn't think that I was, but I might be. Then what kind of damage would my meddling do, not only in Connor's relationships with Uncle Ben and Jimmy but also in his relationship with me?

I wasn't prepared to risk it. Uncle Ben and Jimmy would just have to take care of themselves. Connor was family. All of it that I had left.

Chapter 13

That night, after all the dinner dishes had been cleared, cleaned, and put away, I went up to Rachel's room to do some homework and finish putting away my things. As Aunt Esther had promised, Rachel had boxed up all her personal belongings, and I now had the dresser, the closet, and the shelves all to myself. Aunt Esther had told me at dinner that I could choose new wallpaper and bedding if I wanted to, but I didn't think that I did. Rachel's red, black, and white had grown on me, and the room felt comfortable. It didn't feel like mine, but I doubted that new wallpaper or a different color comforter would change that.

The house was a lot quieter now that the holidays were over and Judah and Rachel were gone again. Back to college. Rachel in Oregon. Judah in Minnesota. It surprised me that I noticed their absence as much as I did, since I hadn't spent a lot of one-on-one time with either of them. I missed them. A lot. Especially Rachel.

Aunt Esther did too. She said as much, but that wasn't all. She was still preparing meals for the masses instead of just the five of us. She spoke often to Uncle Ben about what they might do—what we might do—during the summer. She sat alone a lot in front of the window doing nothing at all.

Wondering if that's what she was doing now, and since I didn't feel like sitting alone in Rachel's room for one moment longer, I turned off the light and went downstairs.

My aunt was sitting alone in the front room, but she wasn't doing nothing. The book she'd been reading before the holidays interrupted her was open in her lap. I wasn't going to bother her, but she shut the book when she saw me and motioned to me to join her.

I was glad to.

"Have you gotten all your things put away?" she asked me.

"Not yet."

She smiled. "It'll come, Brenna."

"Yeah."

"I know the room isn't as big as your room at home."

I shrugged. That wasn't the problem.

"And that *that* room was *your* room," she said. "Your space. In your house."

I didn't say anything. I didn't have to. As usual, she had pinpointed my exact thoughts.

"It'll come," she said again.

I wasn't sure that I believed her. "Where's Uncle Ben?"

"He and Nathan went to play racquetball." She set her book on the table beside her chair. "Ben invited Connor, but—"

"He didn't want to go." I wasn't surprised.

"He's in on the computer," she said.

For a moment, the briefest fraction of one, I considered confiding my suspicions about his invitation to his friend Jimmy. He'd gotten permission at dinner. "Do you think that'll come too, Aunt Esther?"

With a slow nod she said, "It may take longer."

We both laughed a little.

We spoke for a while after that about the book she was reading, about how I was enjoying the youth group, about the snowmobiling trip Uncle Ben was planning for Connor and me. We decided that a bowl of popcorn would make the evening perfect, and I followed her to the kitchen and talked more with her while she prepared it.

We'd just gotten back into the living room and made ourselves comfortable when Uncle Ben and Nathan came in the front door, letting in a rush of icy air.

I pulled one of the throws off the back of the couch and wrapped myself in it. Then I ate a handful of popcorn.

Uncle Ben pushed the door shut. "It's getting nasty out there."

"Snowing?" his wife asked.

He nodded.

"So who won?" I had to know.

"They play for exercise," Aunt Esther said. "And for the time together. Not because it matters who wins."

Uncle Ben laughed. "Nathan won. And it does matter."

"Oh, don't worry, Dad," Nathan said. "When you get old enough and start crippling up, I'll feel sorry for you and let you win again."

"I'll be winning before then, thank you. And on my own." He hung his coat and Nathan's in the front closet and crossed the room to sit beside his wife, who leaned against him and took his hand. "When I get old enough and crippled up, he'll feel sorry for me!" He shook his head and then consoled himself with a handful of popcorn from Aunt Esther's bowl.

Aunt Esther laughed and pushed his hair back from his forehead with her fingers. "I do see some gray in there, Ben. You—"

"That's it." He teasingly shoved her aside so he could stand up. "I have a sermon to work on." He snatched another handful of popcorn. "Too bad I'm going through the minor prophets on Wednesday nights. I'm thinking something about respect might be more in order this week."

This was one of the things I'd come to most enjoy about living with my aunt and uncle. They spent a lot of time like this. Sitting together. Talking. Joking around. With nothing in particular on the agenda. With no agenda. Period. I realized that I could probably count on one hand the number of times my parents and Connor and I had done that in our home. Our family had spent a lot of time together, but we always had to be doing something. Watching a movie we'd rented. Working on a project around the house or at the ranch. Going into town to shop. Planning our vegetable garden. Evaluating Connor's or my report cards. Playing pinochle.

Not that there was anything wrong with that. My family had grown close that way. It's just that it was strengthening, somehow, to be with one another. Calming.

Aunt Esther was smiling up at Uncle Ben when I looked up from my bowl of popcorn. "Well, are you the pastor, or are you the pastor?"

"I am the pastor. And it's Micah this week."

"Connor's on the computer," she told him quietly, her smile gone, and I did not miss the apprehension in her tone.

Uncle Ben didn't miss it, either. "He's fine. I'm not even close to ready to put in the final draft." He found his Bible, tucked it under his arm, and went upstairs.

"He goes way too far out of his way for Connor," Nathan said. He sat beside me and helped himself to some of my popcorn. "No offense, Brenna."

I shrugged.

"I don't see how that concerns you, Nathan," Aunt Esther said.

"It makes me mad," he said. "That's how it concerns me."

"Because your father wasn't as lenient with you and Rachel and Judah?"

"No, Mom," Nathan said. "I know he has to be different with Connor and Brenna." He glanced cautiously at me, trying to determine, I suspected, if I resented him mentioning me.

I didn't resent it. I didn't appreciate it, necessarily. But I didn't resent it. "We're not his kids," I said for him, since he was visibly uncomfortable about doing it even though it was the obvious conclusion to his thought. "And he can't just treat us like we are and always have been."

"Right."

"So what's the problem?" Aunt Esther asked him.

"Mom, if you or me or anyone else in this house was on the computer and Dad needed it to work on his sermon—"

"He said he doesn't need it. Are you thinking he was lying?"

"No. Okay." Nathan thought for a moment. "What about that Sunday he stayed home from church because Connor wouldn't—"

"He would never have put up with that from you." Aunt Esther smiled. "You're right. You have to remember that your father has had seventeen years with you. He's built a relationship with you. You know his boundaries, and he knows yours. There's none of that with Connor. And Connor isn't three or four. He's fourteen. He already thinks the way he thinks. He's not going to just snap into our family like a puzzle piece and fit perfectly. He has no desire to do that. He liked his family the way it was, and he thinks it was stolen from him. He—"

"He could try a little. That's all I'm saying." Nathan leaned forward with his elbows on his knees. "It's not like he can get his family back by rejecting this one."

"I know," Aunt Esther said. "But anger clouds things, Nathan. It makes you see answers where there aren't any and despise the ones that are right in front of you." Then she gently reminded him that he knew that.

"But Brenna's trying," Nathan countered after he'd thought about what his mother had said.

"Connor and I are put together different," I said. "That's all."

Nathan stared at me and then slowly turned to look at his mother. "Like Judah and me. Put us in the exact same situation, and we'll have completely different responses."

Aunt Esther nodded.

"For example," Nathan said, "I'd have asked Rebekah to marry me by now if I were Judah."

"Ah, but you're not Judah, are you?" Aunt Esther grinned.

"Nope. But I'm betting Rebekah's wishing he was a little more like me right about now."

"He's getting around to it," I said carelessly and then hurried to shut my mouth. Nathan and Aunt Esther were both looking at me as if my comment had convinced them that I knew something they didn't—which I might. But I wasn't even supposed to mention that Judah had talked to me, let alone what we had talked about.

That didn't mean, however, that I couldn't enjoy pestering their curiosity.

"Did he say something to you?" Nathan asked me.

"I can't say."

"Brenna!" This came from Aunt Esther.

I wasn't at all sorry, but I assured them that I was.

"Yeah, right." Nathan leaned against the back of the couch and pouted while he ate what was left of my popcorn.

When she saw that her son had emptied my bowl, Aunt Esther stood and reached for it, saying she'd refill it if I was still hungry. I wasn't. She nodded and smiled down at me when Nathan handed the bowl to her, and she set it inside her own. "He's getting around to it, you said?"

"Yeah," I admitted slowly. "Something like that."

She said, "Hmm," and left the room.

"She loves Rebekah," Nathan whispered to me. "She and Dad both do . . ." But then something else occurred to him. I could see it in his sudden change of expression from thoughtful to comically perturbed, and he made no effort to hide the fact that his supposed annoyance had everything to do with me.

"What?" I had to work very hard to keep a smile from my lips.

"Why does my brother talk to you and not me?"

A fair enough question. But I had no intention of telling him that it was only because he wasn't a girl. That would give too much away. And it would spoil my fun.

I grinned and stood up. "Good night, Nathan."

Chapter 14

I'd been out of bed for nearly three hours Saturday morning when someone knocked lightly at the door. I shut the drawer I'd just filled with my long-sleeved shirts and got stiffly to my feet. Those shirts were the last of my clothes to be put away, and I'd already arranged my books and pictures on the shelves. I'd hung a couple of posters on the walls and tacked up the horse calendar that Dad had given me. I still had some figurines and my jewelry boxes to arrange on top of the dresser, but for the most part the room was finished. I hurried to straighten the comforter before opening the door, but I needn't have bothered. It was just Connor.

"Morning," he said.

I gave him a quick hug and asked him if he'd slept well.

"Well enough," he said. "I was getting stuff put away, and I found this." He held up his hand and unclenched it slowly to reveal a tiny wood carving that I recognized instantly. A grizzly bear standing on its hind legs with its front paws scratching at the sky. Dad had carved it. "Grandpa put it with my stuff by mistake," Connor said. "Do you want it?"

I shook my head. "You keep it. Grandpa must have wanted you to have it."

"Yeah, well, I don't want it." He held it out to me. Pushed it out to me.

"Connor, trust me." I folded his fingers back around the bear and held his hand still in both of mine. "Wrap it up. Put it away for now. Someday you'll be glad you have it, and you can get it out then." I paused to search his eyes, his features. All I saw was anger. And I could feel it too, in the way his hand was shaking around the tiny bear. "Please. Trust me."

"I said I don't want it," he repeated quietly.

"All right." I allowed the bear to be placed in my hand. "I'll put it away for when you ask me for it."

"Whatever." He wiped his hands on the front of his jeans as if he'd rid them of something dirty. Then he shoved them in his pockets. "The room looks nice," he said.

"Thanks."

"I better go finish mine. Jimmy will be here soon."

I nodded, but then I touched his arm as he turned to leave. "You, uh, you know I love you." It wasn't a truth we frequently verbalized, but the distress in his eyes—it had been there just for a flash of a second—when I'd taken the bear from him persuaded me to do so now.

"Yeah." He kept his back to me. "I know that."

I stood in the middle of the room and watched my brother walk out the door. Only after he'd pulled it shut behind him did I reopen my hand and look again at the wooden bear. It was beautiful. Intricate. I remembered when Dad had carved it. We'd gone to the Boulder River to do some fishing, but it had rained. Dad had picked up a stick and, while we sat in the cab of his pickup waiting for the shower to pass over, had crafted it into the bear with his pocketknife. He'd seen to the finishing details with his smaller tools at home, but he'd whittled that stick into a griz while Connor and I watched and talked about bait. I couldn't understand why Connor wouldn't want it, even considering the things Aunt Esther had said to Nathan about anger. It didn't make sense to me. The bear was a treasure. A memory. So much a piece of who our father had been.

And maybe that was the problem. While I might be learning to find comfort and nearness to my parents in things that had been theirs, Connor obviously was not. To him, they were only reminders of all he had lost. Reminders he clearly wasn't ready to contend with. Reminders he resented.

Now.

I cut a corner out of one of my flannel drawer liners and wrapped the bear. Then I placed it between two nightshirts that I never wore and shut the drawer. It would be safe there until Connor asked for it and accessible to me in the meantime should I want to hold it close.

For the next half hour I pulled things out of the most recent box Grandpa had sent and placed them on the dresser. One wood jewelry chest, one glass heart-shaped one. Three ceramic bunnies that Mom and I had painted when I was seven or eight. A chunk of amethyst that I'd purchased at a rock shop that some old man had in his garage in Billings. Dad had worked a rodeo there one weekend a couple years back. A painted vase with six silk roses in it. A bottle of perfume. My plastic tote of hair accessories— which I'd really been missing. When the box was empty except for those annoying plastic peanuts, I closed it, squeezed it and myself out into the hallway and down the stairs, and tossed it onto the other boxes near the back door.

"Good morning, Brenna." Uncle Ben called to me from the kitchen when I walked by it on my way back to the stairs. He laughed a little, probably because it almost wasn't morning anymore and I was still in my sweats and hadn't been down for breakfast yet. "I'm about to start getting lunch on the table," he said. "Are you hungry?"

"Yeah." I stood at the bottom of the stairs, debating whether or not I needed to go up and get dressed before joining him. I glanced in the mirror hanging above the telephone table. I'd braided my hair right out of the shower before going to bed, and it still looked tidy. My sweats were sweats, but they weren't wrinkled or sloppy looking. And it was Uncle Ben. He'd been known to lounge around in sweats on a Saturday morning—although I could see in the mirror that he was dressed now, tie and all. My curiosity about where he might be heading quickly outweighed my concern about what I looked like. I went to the kitchen and sat at the table. "Are you working today?" I asked him.

"No." He shook his head. "Our ministerial association is meeting this afternoon."

"Ministerial association? What's that?"

"That," he said as he pulled a package of thawed ground Italian sausage out of the refrigerator, "is a group of local ministers—those who want to participate, anyway—who meet together once a month to talk about things and pray together."

"Things?"

"Things," he said. "Like joint services some of the churches might be holding or events going on in the community that we as clergy might want to take a stand for or against." He crumbled the sausage into a frying pan and lit the burner underneath it.

"Sounds a little boring," I reflected.

Nathan came into the kitchen and grabbed an orange from the basket of fruit on the counter. "Pastors need encouraging sometimes too, Brenna." He sat across from me at the table.

Some words of my father's intruded on my thinking as I considered Nathan's statement. Horses are difficult, but a guy can understand them. Not people. And all that right and wrong. No, sir. Ben's crazy.

My uncle wasn't crazy. He was probably the single most sincere person I'd ever met. But I didn't envy him his job. Not when I really stopped to think about it. I got up and stood beside him at the stove. "Is there anything I can help you do?"

"Uh . . . boil some spaghetti? I'll go ahead and stir this meat into the sauce and then we can eat." He grimaced. "I was supposed to do this a long time ago. You won't tell, will you?"

I laughed and crossed my heart. "Not a word." I lifted the lid on the white pot simmering on the back burner. Steam thick with the smell of tomatoes, garlic, and oregano pushed up at me. I glanced at Uncle Ben in surprise. "Did you make this?"

"No," he said. "I'm just the official stirrer. Stirring I can do. Remembering to add the meat at the right time is something else entirely." He smiled. "Esther put it on this morning before she left to pick up Mary."

"Rebekah's mom?"

"Yes. They're cleaning Edna Avery's house. She just got out of the hospital and isn't supposed to do much."

I remembered seeing the sign-up sheet at church. Meals. Cleaning. "I'd have gone and helped," I said.

Uncle Ben leaned toward me, smiling. "I'm sure Rebekah would have too. But Mary had something she wanted to talk to your aunt about. Alone. And Edna lives quite a ways out of town."

"Hmm. A certain upcoming wedding, maybe?"

"Who's engaged?"

"Oh, Dad," Nathan said. "Like it has to be official for it to be obvious."

Uncle Ben shrugged. "I'm just saying I've been in the ministry a long time and nothing's official until it's official, and even then it can be broken."

I laughed, but suddenly felt a little scared for Judah. What if he decided he didn't want to marry Rebekah? Or what if she decided she didn't want to marry him? All these other people—except Uncle Ben—were living their lives as if their wedding was a foregone conclusion. A predestined from the foundation of the earth sort of thing. And it might not be. Things could change.

I reached into the cupboard for the package of spaghetti.

Connor came downstairs twenty minutes later, just in time to help get the dishes on the table. The four of us ate lunch mostly in silence until Uncle Ben said, "I've been looking at some back-country maps, and I think I found a great place to take you two snowmobiling."

Connor looked up from his food. "Are we going to borrow Dr. Teale's machines again?"

"Already asked him. How does next weekend sound?"

"Excellent," Connor said.

"Are you going where we usually go?" Nathan asked his father.

"No. I thought we'd try somewhere new."

"Too bad he only has three snowmobiles." Nathan folded his piece of garlic bread in half and dragged it through his leftover sauce.

"I could rent one for you," Uncle Ben offered. "There's room on the trailer."

Nathan looked at his father as he chewed his bread. Then he looked from Connor to me, then to Connor again, and finally back to his father. He grabbed his plate in both hands and slid his chair back to stand up. "You know what? I've already got stuff going on next weekend."

I smiled at my cousin. I didn't think that he was lying, exactly, but I was pretty certain that the "stuff" he was referring to could easily be rescheduled or even left undone and that he'd simply settled on granting his father and Connor and me the time alone together.

Time that we could definitely use, I had to admit. Especially Connor and Uncle Ben.

Nathan started to say something after he rinsed off his plate, but the sound of the doorbell silenced him.

Connor jumped up from his chair and barely caught his glass of iced tea before it tipped over. "That'll be Jimmy."

Chapter 15

I let my breath out slowly when Connor brought Jimmy into the kitchen. His "Satan" T-shirt must have been in the laundry. He was wearing a plain white one.

"Jimmy," Connor was saying, "this is my cousin Nathan. You know my sister Brenna." He paused while Jimmy mumbled something to me about looking great in gray, then he introduced him to Uncle Ben.

"Hey." Jimmy grinned as he shook Uncle Ben's outstretched hand. "It's the Rice Man."

Uncle Ben let go of Jimmy's hand, and I could see that he was working to keep his face expressionless.

"No, Jimmy," Connor said with a smirk. "This Uncle Ben is a Pastor Man."

"Wow," Jimmy said. "So you're, like, into all that God worship and all that, man?" But he must not have really been asking because he didn't pause for Uncle Ben to answer. "What if our whole world and all of us in it are just part of some giant video game?"

This inspired a questioning look from Uncle Ben.

"Yeah," Jimmy said. "Or like pawns in some monster chess game between two buggy-eyed aliens?"

Nathan shook his head and muttered, "What if you got a brain?" He brought his plate to the counter and then left the room.

I couldn't help laughing aloud. I didn't want to offend Jimmy, or Connor. But . . . was Jimmy serious?

"You think that's funny?" Jimmy said to me. "What if a big ball of intergalactic sludge—"

"Excuse me," Uncle Ben said. He stared right at Jimmy. "How about I ask you something?"

Connor obviously didn't like that idea. "We're going to—"

Jimmy interrupted Connor. "It's your house."

"What if there is a God?"

Jimmy looked at the floor, at the table leg, at Connor's unfinished lunch.

But Uncle Ben kept looking right at Jimmy. "One who loves you?"

Now Jimmy snapped his head up to look at Uncle Ben. "That's a great line, Pastor Man, but that's all it is." Then he turned to Connor. "Where's your room?"

"Nice work," Connor whispered harshly at Uncle Ben as he pushed by him and out of the kitchen ahead of Jimmy.

Uncle Ben watched them go and then went to the sink to begin rinsing dishes.

I grabbed a towel and stepped up to help him. "Are you mad? Connor's just—"

"No."

"Tired?" I tried again because that's how he looked suddenly.

"Tired? I don't know that that's the word either." He reached up to rub the back of his neck. "I do know one thing."

"What's that?"

"The ministerial association is going to have to meet without this Pastor Man today. I have one, possibly two, very lost young men in my house, and I can't just walk away from that." He left the unwashed dishes on the counter and went to the top of the stairs where I heard him talking with Connor and Jimmy. After a few minutes, the three of them walked to the living room and started getting into their coats.

I walked in behind them.

Uncle Ben undid his tie, slipped it off, and handed it to me. "We're going to go look for snowmobiling gear for Connor," he told me. "Do you want me to grab a snowsuit for you while we're there? Or is it better if I leave that for you and Esther?"

I gave him a quick hug. "I'll go with Aunt Esther."

Which is what I did. But not until Thursday after school.

"I'm sorry I couldn't take you earlier in the week," Aunt Esther said as we backed out of the driveway. "It's been a busy few days. Pulling into the driveway to pick you up just now is the first I've seen the house since I left to meet Ben for lunch."

I nodded.

"If we can't find anything you like, Brenna, I—"

"I already talked to Stephanie," I told her. "I can borrow her snow pants and ski jacket." I smiled. "In fact, why don't I just plan on doing that, and you and I can go shopping with nothing in mind?"

She closed her eyes for a second before putting her car in gear and pulling forward. "That sounds wonderful, Brenna. We can look in the bookstore, and—"

"And eat a hot pretzel."

She smiled. "We can eat dinner. Just you and me. I told Ben I might not be home, so he's planning to fix something for himself and the boys."

"Nathan and Connor went back to the school after they brought me home," I said. "There's a JV basketball game or something that Nathan wanted to go to. They're just going to pick up hamburgers later. I left a note for Uncle Ben."

"Great," she said. "Then there's absolutely no guilt. Ben's as good a cook as I am."

I found that hard to believe.

"Anyway," she said, "he won't starve."

We laughed.

"How is school going?" she asked me when we'd driven several blocks without talking.

"Fine." I hated to give her the stereotypical *I don't want to talk about this* one-word response, but there really wasn't much else to say. School was fine. Nothing more. Nothing less.

"Are you making friends all right?"

"Oh, you know. I talk to people. They talk to me. Kids are nice. But I wouldn't say I'd made any friends yet."

"It takes time," she said.

"Yeah."

"How about Connor? How's he doing?"

I laughed. "He's got friends."

"Hmm. I heard about Jimmy."

"Did you?" I would have loved to have been there to overhear that conversation. "He talked to me at lunch today, Aunt Esther. After Connor had gone."

"Did he?"

"Yeah. He wanted to know if I believe all the stuff Uncle Ben told him about Jesus when they were shopping Saturday." I paused when we stopped at a red light, and I watched a mother struggling to navigate her stroller across the rutted snow to the other side of the street. "I told him I did."

"What did he say?" Aunt Esther wanted to know. The light had gone green, and we were moving again.

"I think he's really curious." I looked at her. "He was asking if I thought Uncle Ben would talk to him again. Just him. Without Connor."

"I'm sure he would."

I smiled. "That's what I said. I feel kind of bad for Connor though. It's like he's being left out, or something."

"You can't force someone to be interested in God."

"I know. But Jimmy is Connor's friend."

"Who deserves to at least hear the truth about God, Brenna." My aunt's tone was intense. "If he's even the slightest bit open—"

"I know," I assured her. "I just feel bad for Connor."

"Well," she said, "nothing might come of it. And, if Jimmy does make some changes in his life, it might start Connor doing some thinking too."

"I don't know," I said. "He's pretty bitter. I think he's mad at God. I think he feels that God let him down. That He's undependable and untrustworthy. Maybe he doesn't even believe in God anymore. That's what he keeps saying."

Aunt Esther nodded. She'd heard it plenty of times herself. "But God can still reach him. Even behind all that anger."

"I hope so." It was all I could say without starting to cry.

Aunt Esther and I shopped for three hours and then chose a Mexican restaurant for dinner. Even though I had spent a lot of time with and around her during the past two and half months, I never tired of her ability to be and to have fun. It impressed me because her life had not been, and still was not, without difficulties. She was gracious. And genuine. And even when she was visibly upset, she had this quiet confidence about her that made me feel safe. Like things were going to be okay. Maybe not right this minute, but eventually. It was a strength I'd come to count on in her—more and more as I watched it in action. A strength I hoped I'd observe in myself someday.

The driveway was empty and the house dark when we got back. My note to Uncle Ben was still on the kitchen table, exactly where I'd left it. It was nearly 9:00, so Aunt Esther was understandably concerned. "It's times like this I wish we had an answering machine," she muttered to herself as she set her purse on the table.

"Why don't you?" I asked her.

"You know, I don't know." She smiled. "I guess we've just never gotten one. Ben hates them. He has one in his office at the church, so . . . I wonder if he's still there." She picked up the phone and dialed it. While she waited with it at her ear, she said, "He's been known to have a long Thursday now and again." After a moment—I guessed it to be long enough for about four rings and a *Hello, this is Pastor Ben Ewen*— she set the phone down.

I couldn't help laughing. "Let me guess. You got his answering machine?"

She smiled. "Yes."

"And don't you just hate it?" I teased.

She pointed at me. "You are starting to sound like your uncle."

A car pulled into the driveway. We heard it and saw its lights in the window. Aunt Esther went quickly to the living room and pulled open the front door.

Nathan came in first, said hello to his mother, and handed her two sacks of food so that he could take off his boots. Connor came in behind him.

"There were actually two games," Nathan explained. "Sorry we're so late. I called, but nobody was here." He took the sacks from his mother and joined me in the kitchen. "Are you hungry, Brenna?"

I groaned. I hadn't wanted to waste that last half of that second enchilada. "No."

"Where's Dad? I didn't see the van."

"I was just about to ask you that," Aunt Esther said.

Nathan bowed his head for a silent second and then bit into his hamburger. "Did you try the church?"

"Not there."

"Ah, he was probably pouting because we'd all abandoned him, and so he went somewhere with Pastor Cahill."

"Racquetball?" I suggested.

Aunt Esther shook her head. "Rick doesn't play. But they could have gone to eat. I'll call Mary."

"Don't worry, Mom," Nathan said around another bite of hamburger.

She grinned at him as she put the phone to her ear again. "Don't talk with your mouth full." Her grin disappeared as she hung up. "Answering machine."

"Maybe someone at the church had an emergency or something, Aunt Esther," Connor said.

We all looked at him. Connor rarely joined in on family discussions, and when he did, it was usually only to insert something rude.

"That could be."

"If it is," Nathan said, "Dad will call you. He's probably been trying, or he's been waiting until he knew you'd be home."

"You need an answering machine," Connor said.

Aunt Esther and I looked at each other and laughed.

"What's so funny?" Connor asked.

Another car pulled into the driveway.

"Oh, there's Ben." But as Aunt Esther walked toward the door to open it for her husband, someone knocked at it.

I tried to convince myself that Uncle Ben had simply forgotten his keys, but it was useless. If he'd driven here, he hadn't forgotten his keys.

Nobody would drop by to say "Hi" at this hour, right? Right.

My stomach began to feel as if someone was stepping on it.

But I was being ridiculous. I had to be. Jumping without cause back to the memory of when the highway patrol officer had come to the ranch to tell us about Mom and Dad's accident.

He'd pulled into the driveway. Late.

And he'd knocked at the door.

Chapter 16

When I saw Pastor Cahill and Uncle Ben in the doorway, I shut my eyes for a second, sat heavily on the nearest chair, and forced myself to breathe. Then I looked at Connor. He'd set his hamburger down. The color had gone from his face. I reached across the table and squeezed his hand.

He squeezed mine back.

It's okay, I told myself. It wasn't happening again.

But I felt as if I could throw up.

"I'm sorry, Esther," Pastor Cahill was saying. "Uh, his keys are . . . are at the church."

"Ben?"

The concern in Aunt Esther's voice troubled me. I got to my feet and went to the living room, only vaguely aware of Nathan and Connor close behind me.

"Ben, are you sure you don't want me to stay? I can tell them—"

"No," Uncle Ben said to Pastor Cahill. "Rick, thank you. You and Mary go home. It's . . . I'm okay."

"All right." Pastor Cahill looked about as comfortable with this suggestion as Dad had looked the first time I'd tried to persuade him that I was old enough to date. Unlike Dad, though, Pastor Cahill kept his opinion to himself. He pulled open the door. "Esther," he said, "if you need anything, if he needs anything, call me. It doesn't matter what time it is. You know that."

Aunt Esther nodded and slowly shut the door. "Ben?" She stepped near her husband again, but seemed reluctant to touch him. His face was colorless and expressionless. His hair was a mess. And his eyes . . . I'd seen the look in his eyes before. In my own eyes when I'd stopped in front of a mirror by accident after Mom and Dad's funeral service. The vacant look I'd seen staring back at me then had frightened me. And it was even more unsettling to see it in someone else's eyes because I knew what it meant.

Uncle Ben was spent.

Gently, Aunt Esther's hand went to his face. "What happened?"

He opened his mouth a couple of times, but no words would come. Finally, he lifted his hand to her shoulder, pulled her close to him and clung to her.

"Ben, you're shaking," she said.

"I'm a little cold," he said.

"Come sit down."

He nodded.

Aunt Esther led him to the couch. "Let's get your coat off," she said.

He nodded again, but didn't move to do it.

So Aunt Esther pulled it off.

The shirt he was wearing was not his. It was a dress shirt, like the white one he'd left the house in, but this one was navy. And too big for him.

"Ben, please." Aunt Esther placed her hand firmly on his shoulder and pressed a couple of times at it to get him to sit down. When he did, she sat beside him. "Tell me what happened."

He folded his arms across his stomach and leaned forward. "This guy was parked at the church when I got back after lunch," he said. He was looking so completely at Aunt Esther that I wondered if he'd even seen Nathan, Connor, or me. "He gets out of his car, shakes my hand, says I'll never know how glad he is to finally meet me, and then asks me if I have some time to talk with him. I figure I've got a little while before my next counseling appointment, so I say sure, and we go inside. He starts telling me about his wife. And pretty soon he gets around to accusing me of counseling her to leave him, and telling me how this has ruined his life. I don't recognize the names. I don't remember any of the details he's telling me, but he's telling me and getting pretty upset. I tried to keep him calm, but he was losing it, so I reached for the phone to call . . . I don't even know who I was thinking I was going to call. He saw me move. He pulled out a handgun and fired it. Twice. All the while yelling, 'Don't you touch that! Don't you dare touch that!' "

Slowly Uncle Ben rolled up his right sleeve, which was unbuttoned and had been hanging loose over his hand. From the middle of his hand to his elbow, his arm had been heavily bandaged. "One of the shots, the second one, hit me."

Suddenly, my knees felt weak. I had to sit down. I walked to the rocking chair and lowered myself onto it. Uncle Ben had been shot? At the church?

Connor came and stood beside me.

"I'm all right," Uncle Ben assured his wife. Then he went silent.

"Ben?" Aunt Esther waited for him to look at her. "What . . . what happened after that?"

"I sat back down in my chair, and he came around and got right in my face with his gun."

"Oh, Ben."

"All I could think was that there was nobody else in the building. For at least another ten or fifteen minutes. This guy's going to kill me and walk out of here. Ron Baxter is going to come in and find me . . . But the guy didn't do anything. He stood there for a while; it seemed like a long time, but I'm sure it was only a few minutes. Then he started yelling. Yelling at me that I was about to understand how it feels to have my life ruined by somebody I don't even know. Over and over again. That's what he's saying. I can smell metal. I didn't know what he was going to do, and I wasn't going to be able to do anything to stop it, whatever it turned out to be."

"Ben," Aunt Esther said, "It's all right. You're all right."

I could see his hand shaking. And the muscles in his face. But he continued. "The guy stopped yelling, pulled the gun out of my face, and . . ." He squinted his eyes shut and shook his head. "It happened fast, Esther. He put the gun to his own head, and I didn't doubt his intention to use it."

This time, Aunt Esther didn't try to hurry him past his silence.

But Nathan did. "Dad?"

"Right. Sorry. I got up and started telling him all the reasons he didn't want to do this. I don't even remember what I said. I just kept talking until he caved and gave the gun to me."

My stomach was all too quick to seize on the tension of what it might have felt like in Uncle Ben's office during those moments, and I had to put my head to my knees.

"Brenna," Uncle Ben said, "I'm sorry. I should have had you kids leave the room. I wasn't thinking. I'm sorry."

I wanted to tell him that the last person he should be concerned about right now was me. But I didn't get a chance to say it because Nathan started pressing him again for the rest of what happened.

"Basically," Uncle Ben said, still looking over at me, "I called for help and then sat and talked with the guy—or actually, *to* him since he wasn't saying anything anymore—until someone came."

"Wow," Nathan whispered, shaking his head. "Dad, he could have k—"

"How's your arm, Ben?" Aunt Esther asked quickly, and she followed the question with several more. Where had the bullet gone in? Would it heal up fully? Was he in pain?

Uncle Ben reached behind him for his coat and dug around in the pockets with his left hand. "They prescribed stuff," he said. "I think I put them in here."

Aunt Esther found the prescription bottles, three of them, and handed them to him. "I'll get you some water." She walked quickly to the kitchen, taking a moment to squeeze my hand as she passed by me.

When I looked back at Uncle Ben, he was struggling with one of the bottle caps. Though the fingers of his right hand were not bandaged, he wasn't getting any use out of them, and I suspected that he shouldn't be trying to. I stood up and walked around the coffee table to help him. I reached to grab the bottle, but pulled my hand back when I thought better of it. "I hate those childproof caps," I said as I sat beside him.

"Me too."

"Would you like me to try it?"

"Please."

I took all three bottles from him and carefully read each of the labels. Antibiotics. Painkillers. An anti-inflammatory. Strong stuff, all of it. 30 mg every three to four hours.

Aunt Esther arrived then with a glass of water, so I stood up, handed her the prescription bottles and the pills I'd gotten out, and went back to the rocking chair.

"You know what the craziest part is?" Uncle Ben said after he'd handed the glass back to Aunt Esther. "The guy got the wrong church. That's why nothing he said made sense to me. It was actually Bruce Henslin that counseled his wife because apparently the guy got violent with her whenever he took himself off his medication." He leaned back and rubbed at his eyes with the fingers of his left hand. "He got the wrong church."

"Bruce Henslin? He pastors the—"

"That's right. The names of our churches are similar." Uncle Ben sounded almost angry. And like he'd had this conversation already. "That's a mistake you make when you're an out-of-town bridesmaid looking to show up for a wedding rehearsal. It's not a mistake you make when you're going to . . . I'm cold, Esther."

She pulled the throw off the back of the couch, unfolded it, and started to put it over him.

But he shook his head and pushed it away. "I . . . I need a shower."

Nathan went to him. "Come on, Dad. I'll walk upstairs with you."

Uncle Ben stood to go with him, but then he noticed Connor. "We were going to . . . Connor, I can't . . . I won't be able to take you snowmobiling this weekend. We'll go later. We will."

Half-expecting my brother to respond with a rude mumble—or to not respond at all—I stepped toward Uncle Ben and opened my mouth to tell him to not even think about that. But Connor hurried by me and got the words out first.

We stood in the doorway for a long time looking at the stairs after Uncle Ben, Aunt Esther, and Nathan had gone up, and then we went back to the living room. Connor sat on the couch. I sat beside him.

He was the first to speak. "What a psycho."

"No kidding."

"Poor Uncle Ben."

I nodded.

"What a psycho," Connor said again. His tone sounded almost as numb as I was beginning to feel.

I decided it was time to change the subject. "Connor," I said, "thanks for being decent about the snowmobiling trip." I picked up the throw Uncle Ben had pushed away and covered myself with it. "I can't believe he'd even think of that."

So quietly that I almost didn't hear him, Connor said, "I can." He turned to face me. "Brenna, you know Saturday when he took Jimmy and me shopping?"

"Yeah."

"At first I was really mad at him. I thought he was just taking us because he didn't want to leave me alone with Jimmy or he didn't want to have Jimmy in his house or something like that."

"He could have just told Jimmy to leave," I said, "or have taken him home himself."

Connor nodded. "That's what I realized after a while. And he was really good to Jimmy. I mean, you could tell, when he was talking to him, that he really cared about what was going on with him." He grabbed the other throw off the back of the couch, rolled it up in a ball, hugged it to his stomach, and leaned forward against it. "It meant a lot to me that he treated Jimmy that way." He looked at the top of the coffee table. "Especially since I'd really only invited Jimmy over to get on his nerves."

I decided not to reply. It wasn't my place to console him, even though it was true that good things had come about in his mind and Jimmy's in spite of his original hurtful intentions. Nor was it my place to tell him that it was about time he'd recognized what a loser he had been, even though that too might be true.

He could think on things himself for a while.

Chapter 17

Nobody at the prayer meeting in the cafeteria Friday morning was interested in breakfast by the time Nathan finished talking. Not because he'd been graphic. He hadn't. And he hadn't mentioned any specifics that anyone with access to a newspaper couldn't already know. But he had divulged his feelings about what had happened to his father. That he was scared.

"I've never seen him like that," he told us. "And it's not like we've never been through anything bad or ugly. When our friend drowned in Alaska, and we found his body . . . there was nothing pretty about that."

"But you guys were expecting to find what you found," Stephanie said. "Or at least you knew it was a possibility. Your dad went to the church yesterday expecting to do what he always does, and things went crazy. Fast. By the time he came home last night, he'd had to retell what happened, more times than he could count would be my guess. Doctors. The police. My dad. Rebekah's dad. He probably had one or two drugs in his system. There's a huge physical drain that takes place when you lose blood and are in fairly continuous pain." She shook her head. "And that's not even taking into account all the emotional stuff going on inside him. He was probably ready to drop in every possible way. And I doubt he slept well enough last night, even with the painkillers he was on, to remedy it much."

"You're right," Nathan said. "I mean, I know all that. But—"

"But it's your dad," someone across the table from him said.

"Yeah."

"And then there's knowing how easily that guy could have killed Uncle Ben," Connor said. "Or himself in front of Uncle Ben." He shook his head. This was the first time Connor had come with Nathan and me to the cafeteria. I suspected that it was more because he wanted to be near family than because he wanted to pray. But he hadn't been disrespectful to anyone. In fact, he'd been silent until now.

"That's right," Nathan said. "I couldn't sleep last night thinking about that."

"Me neither," I said.

Stephanie pushed her tray forward. "I can't believe you guys are even here today."

"Mom made us come," Nathan said. "She thought it would be better for Dad to have some space."

"It probably is," one of the girls said. "For your dad. But you guys have needs too. Doesn't she know that?"

"My aunt hasn't slept." Connor defended her, and I could tell by the rough way he'd said it that he didn't appreciate the girl's comment. "She's doing the best she can."

"I think we need to pray for you guys."

This had come from Marc Slater. The boy who always prayed so loudly.

I cringed as he walked toward us and stood right behind me so that he could place one hand on Nathan's shoulder and the other on Connor's—they were sitting on either side of me. I felt trapped. I was sure he'd pray even louder than usual today since the need was serious. The thought of everyone looking to see what all the noise was about and seeing me right in the middle of it was enough to put sweat on my hands.

And I didn't want Marc to spit on my head.

But Marc didn't pray more loudly than usual. His words were quiet and surprisingly well chosen.

They, combined with the support I felt from all the other kids around us, and the shame I felt for being worried about Marc spitting on my head, made me cry.

But I wasn't the only one who did.

Nathan, Stephanie, Connor, and I left the cafeteria together several minutes before everyone else. We walked to Connor's classroom first, and then to Nathan's. When Stephanie and I were alone and on our way to her classroom she said, "My dad's going to stop by your house this morning on his way in to the hospital."

"I'm sure Uncle Ben and Aunt Esther will appreciate that."

She nodded.

"Was he there yesterday?" I asked her. "At the ER?"

"It's his second home," Stephanie said as she nodded. "Actually, he's there more than he's home some days."

"That must be kind of hard."

She shrugged. "It's what he does. And he's good at it. He helps a lot of people."

"Did he say anything to you about Uncle Ben's arm? I noticed last night that he couldn't really use his hand all that well."

"The block they gave him before they put in the sutures might have still been limiting him," she said. "But the bullet did glance off his—oh, what did Dad call it?—his ulnar nerve." She held her arm out, palm up, and ran her finger along the side of her forearm closest to her body. "In here somewhere. Dad showed me where on a diagram of the human body with all the nerves and stuff on it, but you know, those things aren't exactly in large print."

I nodded. "Uncle Ben wasn't very specific about any of that," I said. "The bullet went right through his arm?"

"Yeah. Missed the bone. And the artery, fortunately. But it did tear into some muscle, and, like I said, nicked that nerve."

"Will that heal?"

She shrugged. "Nerves don't regenerate, and it was damaged. So Dad says that realistically, and he won't know for sure until a couple of weeks from now when they can do a nerve conduction study, that Pastor Ewen will have anywhere from one to ninety-nine percent disuse of his four fingers. Obviously, he's hoping for the one percent end." She stopped walking in the middle of the hall and turned to look at me. "I can't believe we're even having this conversation. Who would think that a pastor would get shot at work?"

When I offered no reply, she asked another question. A real question. "Does he have someone he can talk to?"

"I don't know."

"Rebekah's dad, I suppose." She adjusted her book bag on her shoulder and started walking again.

"I know Aunt Esther called Judah this morning." I stepped in beside her. "He's going to drive up tonight." I squinted my eyes shut. I was tired, and I couldn't think straight. "Down. He's going to drive down, I mean." I wondered how I was going to survive a whole day at school when I'd had to correct myself about something as simple as the direction one would drive to get from Minnesota to Colorado. Southwest. Down.

Fortunately, I didn't have to try. Shortly before lunch, I was called to the office where Aunt Esther was waiting for me. "Connor and Nathan are already out in the van," she said after I returned from my locker with my coat and books. "Ben and I thought you guys might be tired. I had the secretary leave notes for all your teachers."

I walked beside her through the front doors of the school, down the steps, and along the sidewalk toward the parking lot. "I don't think I had anything important this afternoon," I told her. "No tests, I mean."

"Good."

"Are you all right, Aunt Esther?"

"I'm okay."

When we got to the van, I was surprised to see Uncle Ben sitting in the front passenger seat and to hear him say, "Hey, Brenna," as if it was just a regular day and we were going out for fries and ice cream. He even smiled at me and told me to be sure to buckle up.

I sat beside my brother and buckled up.

"Let me tell you what we're thinking," he said when his wife turned the van out of the parking lot and onto the street. "It's been busy at our house this morning. People mean well, but—"

"You know Mike Leothke?" Aunt Esther cut in. "He goes to the church. Owns a construction business?"

Nathan, who was sitting behind Connor and me, leaned forward. "Yeah?"

"He came by the house this morning and handed us a cell phone, a map with directions on it, and the key to his cabin in the foothills." Aunt Esther adjusted the heat control. It had gotten too warm in the van. "He said we could use it or not. It was up to us."

"Sounds good to me," Nathan said.

"Me too," Connor agreed.

Uncle Ben looked over the back of his seat at me. "Brenna?"

I smiled. "I don't have any pressing plans. But what if someone needs to get hold of you?"

"Anyone who might has the cell phone number," he said. "Everyone else can call Rick, and he'll tell them what's up. We called and left the directions with Judah. It'll add an hour to his trip, but he'll meet us up there."

"Are we going to stay up there all weekend?" Connor wanted to know.

"No," Uncle Ben said. "Just tonight. We'll head home after lunch tomorrow."

Aunt Esther drove us back to the house so that we could drop off our school stuff and pack overnight bags. During the fifteen minutes that we were there, the phone rang whenever someone wasn't already talking on it, and two people dropped by—one with a casserole and the other, a man in a uniform, with the news that the church was no longer a "crime scene," so someone had been hired to clean the pastor's office.

When Aunt Esther shut the door behind that second visitor, she leaned her forehead against the wood and started to cry. I'd just come into the living room with my bag when he had arrived, so I'd heard their whole conversation. I set my bag on the couch and slowly approached my aunt.

"I'm glad someone thought of that," I said.

She nodded and wiped at her eyes.

"Thought of what?" Uncle Ben had come into the living room. When he saw his wife, he walked by me and pulled her close to him. "Esther? Please don't cry. It's going to be okay."

"I know it will, Ben," she said, hugging him back. "Right now doesn't feel all that okay. That's all."

He nodded, kissed her forehead, and pulled away from her. "Are we ready? Let's get out of here."

The phone rang as we were walking out the door.

We kept walking.

Chapter 18

Mr. Leothke's cabin was beautiful. A huge log A-frame with great big angular windows on the north side that looked out onto the valley between two craggy rock mountains. There was no running water or electricity, but Nathan and Connor quickly got to work building a fire in the wood-burning stove that sat in the center of the bottom floor. The living room-kitchen-dining room. The "bedroom" was the loft above us, which was half the width of the house. Though the furnishings were simple, they were comfortable and more than adequate.

"I'm glad they keep the roads plowed," Aunt Esther said as she unpacked some of the food she'd brought. "The van never would have made it in here otherwise."

"If we hadn't traded in the Jeep," Uncle Ben said, grinning, "we'd have been able to get in here regardless."

She leaned over the back of the couch where he was sitting to squeeze his shoulder. "But they do keep the roads plowed, Ben Ewen. So it's a non-issue."

He raised his hand in surrender. His left hand. His right hand was elevated on a pillow in his lap, surrounded by two of those snap-to-activate cold packs. "You're right."

"Of course I am." She kissed his cheek and then recruited me to help make sandwiches.

"So how are we going to wash the dishes?" I asked her as we worked.

She smiled. "You're not going to believe this, but you have to get water from the creek. And, since it's still January, the creek is frozen over. So Nathan or Connor will have to go down there, chop a hole in it with an ax, and bring buckets of water up to the house."

"I think I'll be skipping my shower tomorrow," I said.

She nodded. "We can heat water for any washing that we do need to do."

"In a big pot on top of the wood-burning stove," I said. "We used to have to do that at the ranch when the power was out."

"I remember." She started spreading mayonnaise on the pieces of bread she'd sliced. "I remember the first time I went there. Ben and I were engaged. We'd just come back from our team's second missions trip to South America. He wanted me to meet your grandparents. To see where he'd grown up. I remember driving there from Billings. It seemed to take forever. I couldn't believe we were going all that way and were still in the same state. There were so many miles of—" She shrugged. "Land. No trees, well, hardly any. No mountains. It was Montana. There were supposed to be mountains. Ben had mentioned Eastern Montana frequently enough, but I never knew it was going to be any different from the Montana everyone sees in calendars. And there were no buildings either. Just land and sky." She pulled out a second loaf of homemade bread and handed it to me to slice. "It was beautiful. And when I got to the ranch and had spent a couple of days there, I had never been more amused at God."

"Amused? At God?"

"Yes," she said. "Because He'd put someone like Ben, who'd been raised in a place like that, with someone who'd been raised in Washington, D.C. Our two lives could not have been more different growing up, and yet we were about to get married and build one life together."

"Were you scared?" I asked her.

"About marrying Ben?" She smiled. "No. Not at all. It was only when your grandfather expected me to climb on a horse and help move cattle that I got scared!"

"Did you do it?"

"Yes, I did," she said. "To the great amazement of your grandfather and your father, I did it."

"Uncle Ben wasn't amazed?"

"No," he said from behind us.

"He didn't doubt I'd be able to do it," Aunt Esther explained. "He'd gotten it into his head somehow during the missions trips that I'd always come through for him."

"She does," Uncle Ben said. "She did then and she still does now."

Aunt Esther turned quickly away from me to wipe mayonnaise off her knife with a paper towel. She wiped the knife until it was clean and then kept rubbing. "I wasn't there for you yesterday."

"What?" Uncle Ben looked toward her.

Her eyes were wet with tears when she looked back at him. "I said I wasn't there for you yesterday."

He stood up and walked around the couch to stand right in front of her. Raising his left hand to her chin, he tilted it up so that she'd have to look at him. "Esther, you were exactly where you were supposed to be all day yesterday. And when I got home last night and needed you, you *were there* one hundred percent. And you're here now. And," he smiled a little, "if it ends up that I can't tie my own tie after this, you'll be *there for me* then."

She smiled back. "I'll buy you some of those clip-on ones."

"No, you won't." He lowered his hand to his side again. "You'll have to tie them for me, like you did when we were first married. Before I knew how."

She took his face in her hands and tilted it down so that he'd have to look at her. "I'd be happy to do that. But you're going to be able to tie them yourself."

As I finished slicing the last of the bread, I couldn't help noticing how tired they both looked. I hoped that some food, some quiet, and being here in this cabin would help them relax enough to rest. Maybe even sleep.

When Connor and Nathan came in from the driveway, where they'd gotten into a snowball fight on their way back from the woodshed with a second load of wood, Aunt Esther put the platter of sandwiches on the table, and we sat down to eat. Everyone ate well I noticed, and then we spent the afternoon doing and not doing every kind of nothing imaginable and enjoying it. Connor and Uncle Ben played a game of chess. Aunt Esther read for a while. Nathan took a nap on the couch. I sat in a chair and counted the logs from the fat ones at the base of the house to the thinner ones at the roof. I kept losing count, though, and eventually fell asleep.

When I woke up, the sky outside the windows was gold at the horizon, turquoise above that, and deep blue with night above that. Someone had placed a camp lamp on the coffee table, and its light was warm and surprisingly sufficient for such a large room. Connor and Nathan were hovering over the chessboard now, and Uncle Ben and Aunt Esther were sitting side by side on the couch. He was reading his Bible, and she was leaning against his shoulder with her eyes shut.

I stretched when I stood up, but it didn't help the kink in my neck.

Uncle Ben smiled up at me. "I don't think that chair was constructed with sleeping in mind."

"I suppose not," I said. "Is the outhouse out back?"

"Yeah," he said. "Take a flashlight." He pointed to a shelf near the door where several flashlights had been placed. "You can see it from where we parked."

As soon as I stepped past the door, I knew this was going to be a quick trip and my last one until morning. The night air was icy, but that wasn't the worst of it. Except for my flashlight beam, it was completely dark once I'd gone around the house and into the trees. The snow crunched beneath my boots, and at each step I went in deep, down to my knee. Step after step after step. Wind moved in the branches around me, and snow kept dumping off them onto the ground.

And the outhouse was an outhouse. Nasty even without flies.

I went up to the loft to change into sweats as soon as I got back inside the cabin. I considered staying up there. Lying down on one of the cots and getting a good night's sleep. But I decided not to. I wanted to be near everyone. If I got tired, I could find a place to stretch out down there.

Nathan challenged me to a game of chess even before I'd stepped off the ladder coming down from the loft. I sat across from him at the coffee table and leaned back against the bottom of the couch. "I'm not very good," I told him.

Uncle Ben moved his leg to make more room for me. "Listen to this verse," he said. "It's one we've heard a million times, but . . . well, listen. It's Isaiah 26:3." Then he read, "*Thou wilt keep him in perfect peace, whose mind is stayed on thee: because he trusteth in thee.*" He stayed quiet for a moment. "The note in here about the word *mind* says 'thought or imagination.'" He looked at his wife. "I guess I've never really picked up on that before. Not like now, anyway."

"Thought or imagination," Aunt Esther repeated.

"Yes. See, this is how we're going to get through this."

"What do you mean?" Nathan asked him. He'd lined up all his pawns and was reaching for his pile of back-row pieces.

"Well," Uncle Ben said, "we have to keep our minds on God."

"Yeah, Dad," Nathan said. "We're always supposed to do that." He'd clearly missed the revelation his father was finding so compelling.

As had I.

"Okay, let me get specific. When I shut my eyes and see that guy's face, I have to put my thoughts back on God. When I start wondering if I could have done anything to have prevented him from getting so upset in the first place, I—"

"You don't seriously do that, do you, Dad?"

"Yes, Son. I do. I think that maybe he would never have pulled out his gun if I hadn't reached for the phone. Sometimes I think about how close he was to the edge and what he would have done if—"

"Ben," Aunt Esther said, "you can't do that. It ended—"

"I understand that, Esther." He took in a long breath and let it out slowly. "And that's my whole point. That's what I'm saying. When my mind starts going there, I have to rein it back and make it stay on God. Give whatever's going on in my head straight to Him."

"And then God gives you peace?" I found it hard to believe that it could be that simple. Especially perfect peace.

Uncle Ben nodded. "It doesn't change what happened or what could have happened, and it doesn't mean those thoughts won't be back five seconds from now. But when my thoughts are on Him, I do have peace. It was true even last night. Each time I cleared my head enough to force myself to pray and to remember who He is, there was peace."

"And there's that Scripture about taking every thought captive—'to the obedience of Christ,'" Aunt Esther said. She was working through it as she spoke. Thinking aloud. "And the 'whatsoever things are true . . . think on these things' one."

"A guy could do a sermon on it," Uncle Ben said. He leaned his head back against the back of the couch and shut his eyes.

"You go first," Nathan said to me when he'd finished placing his pieces.

I chose a pawn at random and slid it ahead two spaces.

Nathan moved his king's knight out. "But it is hard to redirect your thinking," he said. "I mean, my mind grabs onto things and runs with them."

"I think that's exactly what Uncle Ben's saying we're not supposed to do," I said. "He's saying that we're in charge of what we think about, and we'd best be thinking on God." I glanced at the Bible on Uncle Ben's lap. "Right, Uncle Ben?"

"You're going to have to ask him later," Aunt Esther said. "He's asleep."

Chapter 19

A nudge at my shoulder and then a sound right at my ear woke me. It took me a moment to remember where I was . . . Mr. Leothke's cabin. I'd fallen asleep with my head on the coffee table, inches from the chessboard. I remembered putting my head down to think about my next move. Nathan was about to slide his rook into position to checkmate my king, but I knew there had to be some way I could block it.

The chess pieces were a mess now. A couple of the pawns were still moving. That had been the sound at my ear. Onyx falling against onyx. Had I knocked the pieces over in my sleep?

At a movement on the couch behind me, followed by a sharp breath, I turned to look at Uncle Ben. He was still sitting where he had been, but he was no longer sleeping. He had pulled his right arm in close to his body and was clutching it with his left hand. His face was strained, and he seemed to be forcing himself to breathe. "I didn't see you there," he said quietly. "Sorry I woke you up."

My having been awakened was the least of my concerns. "Are you all right?"

"I put my hands out to catch myself without thinking," he said.

Then I understood. He'd gotten up, had bumped into me, had lost his balance, and had caught himself with his hands on the coffee table.

"Oh, your arm." I got to my feet. "I'll get Aunt Esther."

"No," he said, almost sharply. "Leave her be. I'd take a cold pack, though, if you'd go get that."

I nodded and went to find one. Dr. Teale had given us a whole bagful of them. Then I brought him a glass of water and his medicine, recalling that Aunt Esther hadn't wanted to wake him when he was last supposed to have it. He accepted the pillow and blankets that I carried down from the loft and even listened to my suggestion that he should lie down and try to get some more rest. But I didn't kid myself. Unless that painkiller had suddenly changed properties, he'd be awake for a while yet with the pain.

"Are you sure you don't want me to get Aunt Esther?"

"I'm sure, Brenna." There was that sharpness again.

"Okay." I placed my hand on his shoulder and then to his neck and face. Cold sweat. "Okay." I slid the coffee table out of the way and pulled over one of the wood chairs. The one I had fallen asleep in earlier. Aunt Esther was curled up with a blanket in the other one—the one with cushions—sleeping. "Is it letting up at all?"

He didn't answer, which was answer enough.

Maybe I could redirect his attention, or at least distract it a little. "I've been thinking about something," I said. If he asked me what, I'd keep talking. Otherwise I'd leave him alone.

"What's that?"

Good.

"I know Grandpa didn't raise you and Dad in the church," I said. "So, how did you, you know, become so . . . so . . . ?"

He smiled. "Obnoxious?"

"No."

"That's the word my father used to use. That, and 'dumber than a wedge.'"

"Well, he doesn't anymore." I shook my head. "No. I was thinking 'committed.' I mean, how did you even find out about God?"

"It wasn't anything dramatic," he said. "No angels while I was on my knees in a field of peach pits or anything like that. I had told this friend of mine about the griz on that backpacking trip I told you about and also about what I'd said to God that night. And he said, 'Well, have you thought about Him since then?' I had to say no. He asked me if I'd like to. I said sure. He told me about Jesus. I believed him."

"That's it?" I was surprised. "What if he had told you Isis was god? Goddess, I mean?"

He laughed. "It wasn't only what he said. It was this peace, this knowledge I had inside while he was talking that what he was saying was true."

"Like Jesus Himself was talking to you too."

"Yes." He looked up at me. "Have you experienced that?"

I nodded. I remembered. But it had happened only once. Right before I'd prayed with my Sunday school teacher. So long ago.

"Judah's not here yet." Uncle Ben's left hand had gone to his arm again.

"I'll let him in," I assured him. Then I noticed a fishing magazine on the shelf underneath the coffee table. I picked it up and began to read softly to him. It was boring, but that was perfect. After a while, a couple of articles, Uncle Ben's eyes closed. And after a longer while, he was breathing easily. I read a few letters from subscribers just to be sure and then shut the magazine and put it away.

Judah got to the cabin a couple hours later. It was almost dawn. I went to the door as soon as I heard the hum of his Jeep.

"Hey, Bren," he said as he stepped inside, and I shut the door behind him. He dropped his bag on the floor and hugged me. "You doing okay?"

"Yeah."

He pulled off his coat and hung it on one of the hooks near the door.

"I'll put some more wood in the stove," I said. It had cooled off in the cabin.

"I'll get it," he said. "Tell me how Dad's doing, Brenna. Really."

"Well," I said, "he was in some pretty serious pain a couple hours ago, but he's been asleep again for a while."

"That's good."

I stared at the camp lamp on the coffee table. "The first night was rough, Judah. Not because of the pain, but . . ." I shrugged. Judah wasn't an idiot. He'd know why it had been rough. In fact, that's probably what he'd been asking about. Tell me how Dad's doing, Brenna. Really.

"It's good he can sleep," Judah said after a while. "I couldn't sleep for more than an hour or two at a time for probably three weeks after Tommy drowned. And then I only did because I was exhausted. Of course, Dad must be on some pretty heavy painkill—"

I shook my head. That wasn't it. "He found a verse in the Bible." I couldn't remember where he had found it, but I did remember what it said. I quoted it to Judah and then told him about the conversation we'd had. "He fell asleep right after that and slept for six hours before—"

"He's looking in the right direction right from the start," Judah said. "I guess he remembers all the stuff he told me, only he's better about actually doing it."

"You were sixteen years old."

"I," he said with a grin, "was a mess."

Judah and I talked for nearly an hour. About the details his mother hadn't told him. About his drive down. About Connor. And about me. How I was and wasn't coping with the loss of my parents. How I liked and didn't like Colorado. How I had, but hadn't really, made friends. How I was trying to look more honestly at and to God but wasn't really seeing Him. By the time we went silent and Judah had finished with the stove, grabbed a blanket and throw pillow, and lay down on the floor near the couch to get some sleep, I'd pretty much concluded that A Mess wasn't all that far off the mark of how I was doing. Really.

But I didn't think about it. I climbed the ladder to the loft, found an empty cot, and fell asleep without even taking time to get comfortable.

Judah stayed in Colorado for four days, and Uncle Ben seemed to emerge from the time with his son with a lot more strength than any of us would have dared to hope for. And he needed it. There were visits with the man who'd come to his office that afternoon, and with his wife, and Bruce Henslin, the pastor who had counseled her. The first time back to the church—to his office. Bad dreams.

But time passed. Two months worth. More of it well than poorly.

Connor's relationship with Uncle Ben and Aunt Esther grew closer and stronger. Whenever Uncle Ben was home, Connor was near him—almost to the point of irritation. But nobody complained. It was such a pleasant turnaround from the way things had been. He'd stopped brooding about having to go to church, though he still didn't talk much about God, and he started coming to youth group too. So did Jimmy.

Uncle Ben went right back to work, keeping all his counseling appointments the Thursday a week after he was shot. He did set up a new schedule with Rebekah's father so that neither of them would spend a lot of time alone in the building.

His arm had not healed up as close to the one percent disuse mark as Dr. Teale had been hoping for. He had some sensation in three of his fingers—none in the little one—but he couldn't get any strength behind them to grip anything, even with the full use of his thumb. So he could do things like direct the steering wheel, but couldn't unbutton a button. Or cut steak. Or tie his tie. And he'd drop his keys now and then. Physical therapy was helpful in that it kept his muscles loose and provided an environment in which he could learn to make adjustments to the way he did things since he was right-handed. But, as Stephanie had already told me, the bottom line was this: Nerve cells don't regenerate—you have to live with it. He was learning to. And maintaining a sense of humor about it too, most of the time.

Aunt Esther was looking forward to having Judah and Rachel home again for a week at spring break, as was Rebekah.

Nathan and Stephanie were preparing to start their final season with the track team, both of them with the goal of winning a state title.

Grandpa and Grandma were planning to drive down for a week or so in May when they figured they'd be able to count on clear roads. They wanted to see Uncle Ben, and us, and to bring down the last of our boxes.

It seemed that everyone was moving forward. Enjoying life. Healing.

Everyone but me.

It wasn't that I was miserable or crying all the time. I wasn't. I got along well enough with everyone, and enjoyed school, and church, and my time at the house. I could welcome memories of my parents and not become upset.

But I felt as if I wasn't living my own life anymore. Almost as if I wasn't even me anymore. I had the same shoulder-length blonde hair. The same brown eyes. The same smile. The same ideas about things. But I was living a different life. The room that I slept in wasn't mine. The house that I returned to each afternoon wasn't home. The people that hugged and prayed with me every night were not my parents. And I hadn't made one single close friend.

I'd called my friend Beth back home, thinking that talking to someone I'd been close to once would encourage me. Make me feel more like myself. But it had accomplished just the opposite. We'd had nothing to talk about, and I'd hung up the phone feeling more disconnected than I had before I'd picked it up.

I shoved the feelings aside as much as I could, though, telling myself that this was a normal stretch of the mostly uphill trail of adjusting. I'd read that phrase in a magazine, and I repeated it to myself often. I tried to do what Uncle Ben had talked about too. Staying my mind on God. I tried to read my Bible. To pray. To sing church songs when I was doing an activity that didn't require much concentration, like washing the dishes.

But I wasn't very good at it.

I knew that I should—and could—talk to Uncle Ben or Aunt Esther about how I was feeling. Or maybe even Grandpa or Grandma. But I didn't want to sound like an ungrateful whiner. My life was fine. Good, even. Besides, it wasn't as if Uncle Ben and Aunt Esther would be able to do anything to change the fact that they were not my parents, and they were already treating me as well as if they were.

This wasn't their fault. Or their problem.

It was mine.

I'd just have to figure it out for myself.

But after school on a Wednesday in mid-March, I had to talk to someone. I'd been given a flyer for the sophomore class annual Bring Your Parents to School Day, and just having that bright green slip of paper in my bookbag knotted up my insides. I dug it out as soon as I got back to the house and took it upstairs to show Connor.

He read it, held it in the air for a moment, and then shrugged and handed it back to me. "So."

"So?"

"Yeah. So."

I sat on the edge of his bed. "First of all, it's the stupidest thing I've ever heard of. What sixteen year old is going to want to be seen with her parents at school?"

"Obviously, that's part of the point. Breaking barriers or something."

"Yeah, well it's stupid."

"You wouldn't say that if we were home and Mom could go with you."

I clutched the paper and didn't reply.

"You could ask Aunt Esther."

"She's not Mom."

Connor thought about that. "I'm sure legal guardians are allowed."

"She's not Mom."

"I have homework, Bren," he said. "And there's church tonight."

I slammed his door when I left. But later, at church, I pulled him aside and apologized. "It was a stupid thing to do." My brother was in the same position as I was, except that the freshman class wasn't putting on a Bring Your Parents to School Day. He didn't have the answer, the miracle solution, the light-bulb-coming-on bit of wisdom that would make everything make sense either.

"It's okay," he said.

"I'll think about asking Aunt Esther," I promised him. "I've got a couple of weeks to decide."

He nodded and headed into the sanctuary to sit down.

I started to follow him, but someone ran up behind me saying, "Hello."

Tony Kramer.

"My dad and I went to an estate sale earlier this week," he said, "and I found this." He held out a framed photograph of what was instantly recognizable as the northern plains adrift in snow. An iced over two-lane highway. Undulating white to the horizon, and flat gray above that. Ice on the power lines at the left of the picture. And in the forefront at the bottom right corner, a buried-to-the-middle green road sign. SIDNEY with an arrow pointing left. And the name of another town underneath that, but only the tops of the first two letters were visible.

I smiled. Maybe that bottom word was CANADA. Or CIRCLE. Or GLENDIVE. I couldn't read it, but I knew the area, and I had to chuckle at the caption in the matting underneath the photograph: Which Way to the Opera House?

"The man said he thought that photo was taken in Montana," Tony said when he saw me reading. "I remembered you mentioning Sidney, so—"

"Yeah," I said. "We didn't live right near there, but we've been there." I smiled. "It's a big town."

"How big?" he asked.

"About six thousand."

He squinted at me. "That's big?"

"For Eastern Montana, yeah."

"Well," he said, "I thought you'd like the photograph, so I picked it up for you."

"Really?" I took it from him and pressed my fingers lightly to the glass. "Tony, that's so—" I closed my mouth.

Sweet. I had almost said sweet to him again!

We started walking toward the sanctuary.

"Does it look like where you lived?" he asked me.

"Pretty much."

"It looks so desolate."

"But it isn't," I told him. "It's beautiful. I mean, yeah, it's flat and treeless and sparsely populated, but the sky is awesome. Especially during summer thunderstorms." Without warning, tears filled my eyes, and I hugged the photograph against my chest.

Tony stopped walking and placed his hand on my arm. "Brenna? I'm sorry. I didn't mean to make you sad."

"It's not you." I shut my eyes and refused to cry. Not one more tear. When I thought I'd forced my emotions back far enough I said, "I love the picture, Tony. I do. I guess I've just been feeling a little homesick lately."

"I'm sure that's normal."

"Yeah, but I thought I was through with this crying like an idiot in public."

"Why should you be?" The sincerity in his voice impressed me. And quieted my embarrassment. "It's not like you're just going to wake up one morning and be over the fact that your parents are gone. I, uh, I should have thought of that."

The fact that he had thought of me at all amazed me. That he'd remembered the name of a town I'd mentioned once. That he'd spotted the photograph in the first place. That he'd bought it. For me. I didn't want him to feel badly. And that's what I told him. "I'm going to hang it as soon as I get back to the house tonight."

"You don't have to," he said.

I grinned at him. "I know that. It's not like I have to worry about you coming up to the room to check to see if I did!" But then I added, seriously, "I want to have it up. It's a great photograph. Thank you."

He smiled and then walked with me down the center aisle to the front row where I said, "See you later" to him and hurried to sit down between Connor and Aunt Esther.

Chapter 20

The parking lot was nearly empty by the time Uncle Ben made it out to the van after the service. "I'm sorry I kept you all waiting," he said. He handed his Bible to Aunt Esther and climbed in. Aunt Esther had already started the engine to get the heater going.

"Good sermon tonight, Dad," Nathan said from his spot in the seat behind Connor and me. He always sat in the back seat. Connor and I always sat in the middle seat. Nobody had suggested it, and we'd never talked about who would sit where. It had just happened. It had become our routine.

I wished I could have agreed with Nathan, but I'd been so preoccupied with thinking about the photograph in my lap that I really hadn't paid attention to the sermon.

Uncle Ben briefly acknowledged Nathan's remark and then said, "Don't you guys want to know who I was talking with—and what about?"

"I've always told the kids never to ask you that, Ben," Aunt Esther said.

"Oh. Good plan."

It took Connor about four seconds to grab the bait. "So, who were you talking to, Uncle Ben? And what about?"

"Remember that snowmobiling trip we didn't get to take?"

I had forgotten about it, but Connor apparently hadn't. He said, "Yeah," right away.

"We're going to go this Saturday. Can you make it this time, Nathan? Because Mike has—"

"No, Dad. Sorry. A bunch of us are going running."

Uncle Ben glanced at his wife.

"Oh, no," she said, shaking her head. "No. I get too cold."

"Okay, then," he said. "The original three it is."

So Friday after school, the original three—Connor, Uncle Ben, and I—loaded our gear into the van, drove over to Dr. Teale's house to hook up the trailer with the three snowmobiles already strapped onto it, and drove out of town toward the mountains. Uncle Ben and Connor had the front seats, and I was in the middle seat behind them.

I watched Uncle Ben's hands on the steering wheel, his right hand in particular, and thought about driving a snowmobile. Handlebars. The throttle. Steering against a slide. "Uncle Ben?"

"Yeah?"

"Have you . . ." I knew what I wanted to ask him but wasn't sure how to word it. He wasn't overly sensitive about his hand, but I didn't want to risk insulting him or making him self-conscious about it if well-chosen words could make the difference. And I knew they could. A lot of people had said things to him about it. He always responded politely, but I'd noticed that certain types of comments made him look, just for a second, away from the person and down at the ground.

I knew he was waiting for me to finish my question, but all I could think was that I wished I'd never opened my mouth.

After a few moments, he came to my rescue. "I was looking at the snowmobiles," he said. "I don't think I'm going to have a problem, but if I do, I may have to double up with one of you on the big one. Is that all right?"

"Yeah," Connor said. He'd been staring out his window and was probably wondering what had made Uncle Ben think of that. "Sure. But you should be fine."

"I think so. But we'll just have to see how it goes. I really don't want to end up on my face in a pile of snow. Or on a rock. Or at the bottom of a tree."

This yanked Connor's attention away from his window, but he didn't say anything. And Uncle Ben didn't seem to notice.

For several miles, we rode in silence. Uncle Ben hummed a tune to himself. "Should I put in a tape?"

"No," Connor said. And then he laughed. "No, thanks."

I leaned forward and rested my left arm on the back of Uncle Ben's seat. "How did you know what I was going to ask you before?"

"You seemed uncomfortable," he said. "And then it occurred to me that you and I have never really talked about this thing with my hand." He shrugged. "It was a guess, really."

"I just didn't want to say it the wrong way."

"I understand," he said. "But don't worry about it. Legitimate questions don't bug me." He looked away from the road for a second to grin at me. "And even if you do bug me, I'll still love you."

I tapped his shoulder and leaned back in my seat, relieved that I had not offended him.

As it turned out, all my concern was for nothing. Uncle Ben had no trouble operating the snowmobile. We spent the evening driving through the trees on the flat ground immediately around Mr. Leothke's cabin, which is where we were spending the night. The man owned a couple hundred acres and had told Uncle Ben that we were welcome to use his cabin again and to snowmobile on his property. Since it was so late in the season, and many of the public areas were already shutting down for the year, Uncle Ben had decided to take him up on the offer. And I was glad. It would be good to have a warm place to retreat to if anyone started getting too cold. And the area, which we'd have all to ourselves, was gorgeous.

In the morning, we prepared to snowmobile in earnest. Uncle Ben made sure all the machines had plenty of gas. Connor built a huge fire in the wood-burning stove so the cabin would still be warm when we returned. And I made a lunch and packed it in a minicooler to strap to the rack on the back of the snowmobile that I was using. But I couldn't find any elastic cords, so Uncle Ben grabbed a yellow nylon rope out of the back of the van.

"This'll work," he said.

"It's a little long." I laughed. "What is it? Fifty feet?"

He smiled. "We'll just have to loop it around a bit." He maneuvered the rope through and around the handle of the cooler and two of the bars on the rack but couldn't quite get his hand to cooperate with him when it came to tying the knot.

"I'll get that," Connor said, reaching for the rope.

Uncle Ben surrendered it with a hasty, "Thanks." He looked a little frustrated but quickly redirected his attention to climbing onto his own machine. "Are we ready?"

We were.

We spent the morning making our way up one of the sides of the valley to get out of the bottom where there were starting to be patches of dry ground. It was a cold day, and the sun was white and bright in an absolutely clear sky. I was glad I had thought to bring sunscreen. I'd gotten one of the nastiest sunburns of my life during a snowmobiling trip. I wished I had thought to bring sunglasses. The bright sun reflecting off the white snow could give a person a headache.

"Is anyone cold?"

We'd stopped in a stand of small tilted trees just on the edge of the tree line. Above us, the mountain rose to the sky in steep white snow and gray rock faces.

"I'm fine," I told Uncle Ben. "Getting hungry, though."

We decided to eat lunch there but didn't linger long about it. The wind was icy, and the small trees offered little protection from it. Having my gloves off long enough to eat a sandwich was just about all I could tolerate. I didn't even bother with my drink.

When we'd finished, and Connor had secured the cooler to my snowmobile again, he looked longingly up the slope nearest us.

"Don't even think about it." Uncle Ben pulled on his gloves and pointed to a huge overhang of snow far above us. "You don't want that coming down on you. And besides that, that's off Mike's place."

"You're right," Connor said. "But it's fun to see how high you can get before your machine just won't climb anymore."

"I know it," Uncle Ben said. "And then you get to turn her around and fly down. But not today."

We drove around at treeline for an hour or so and then went around a knoll and started making our way down a different valley. There were a lot more trees on this side, and the mountain itself was blocking some of the wind. That helped.

"Look!" Connor shouted when we'd gotten about halfway down. He pulled his snowmobile off to the side and waited for Uncle Ben and me to stop our machines beside him. He was pointing at a clear patch of snow, almost perfectly round, that was surrounded by trees. A tiny creek, that was probably much larger in the spring and summer, trickled down the slope and disappeared beneath the snow on the clearing. "I bet it's a pond."

Uncle Ben nodded. "I think you're right."

"Excellent!" Connor stood up on his snowmobile and took off toward it.

"No!" Uncle Ben shouted. "Connor!"

But Connor couldn't hear him over his engine. Either that, or he was ignoring him.

"He can't hear me," Uncle Ben said. Then he looked at me. "Come on."

I followed him through the trees to the edge of the clearing. It was a pond, all right. Covered in snow and cloudy green-gray ice. Connor had already driven out onto it, and Uncle Ben was following quickly after.

He glanced over his shoulder at me and pointed as he yelled, "Stay there!"

I did.

I turned off the engine and stepped onto the ground. The ice near the edge of the pond looked thick. I couldn't see through it. I took a couple of steps out onto it. I'd been on cracking ice before, and I knew what it sounded like. And felt like. I stood still and listened.

Nothing except the snowmobiles.

Connor made it across the pond, pulled up into the trees, and turned around for another pass. He went full speed toward Uncle Ben, who hadn't even reached the center of the pond yet, and waved at him as he passed by. I saw Uncle Ben turn on his seat to yell something to Connor, but I didn't hear him. It didn't look as if Connor did either. He didn't look back.

Seeing that the ice was holding, I hurried back to my snowmobile and climbed on. I might as well have some fun too. There was something about the speed and the flatness of snowmobiling over frozen-over water. No hidden rocks or roots to worry about. No deceptively deep places to get stuck in. No branches in your face.

The only concern was the ice itself. If it would hold.

I hesitated before leaving the shore, looking to Uncle Ben, hoping he'd wave me on. I'd grown accustomed to waiting for Dad to signal me that the ice was okay, and I wanted that assurance now. One time falling through had been one time too many as far as I was concerned, and I never wanted to experience that again. Especially not in a place as remote as this. The cold was brutal. And the weight of your wet clothes. The frustration of grabbing onto the ice in front of you only to have it fall away too. Again and again and again. The fear.

I shook the memory away. Dad had been right there, and he'd gotten me out before I'd even started to shiver.

Uncle Ben didn't wave to me, but then, he wouldn't have any way of knowing I'd be expecting him to. I didn't think I'd ever told him about my little ice-fishing incident. Connor knew about it, though, and he knew I'd been leery ever since. So when he came around Uncle Ben for the second time, he looked along the shore until he saw me and then waved. I could see his mouth moving as he did. "Come on. It's great!"

Licking my lips, which were chapped and windburned by now, I gave the machine some gas and drove out onto the ice.

Chapter 21

"Are you all right with this?"

I'd barely heard Uncle Ben, who'd pulled in alongside me. Both of us had just turned around at the edge of the pond and were heading out toward the center again. I looked at him and nodded. Mom or Dad must have told him. "I'm good."

And I was. Dad had seen to it that I was back out on the ice again right away. Ice fishing was something he loved. Something we did together. He had allowed me the luxury of waiting for him to survey the ice, but he had not allowed me to keep a fear of it.

I waved as I started away from Uncle Ben, daring him with a grin to race me. Connor pulled up alongside him on the other side, and the three of us sped across the pond.

The ride was bumpier than it had been when I'd come across going the other way, so I let loose a bit on the throttle. We had made a lot of tracks in the snow on top of the ice, and the skis were starting to skip on them.

Uncle Ben or Connor would beat me for sure. Connor was already ahead, and Uncle Ben was on a bigger, more powerful machine.

Oh well. Let them beat me. I'd come to have fun, not to rattle out my teeth.

But I got almost to the shore even with Connor and ahead of Uncle Ben. When I turned on my seat to make a face at him about losing to us, my hands went so tight that my machine spurted forward with a jerk that nearly spilled me. I snapped my head around and paid attention to what I was doing just long enough to skid to a stop.

The front of Uncle Ben's snowmobile had broken through the ice. He stood as it went down nose first, gasping at the cold of the water, but his weight as he tried to push himself off only forced the snowmobile further under. Not only did he not get a jump but also his feet slipped on the seat when he tried. He went knees and face first into the water over the front of his now completely submerged machine.

"Connor!" I yelled.

He was hurrying to get his snowmobile turned around. "I don't see him!"

"He went in at an angle!" I knew that I didn't have to tell him what that meant.

Uncle Ben was under the ice.

"No!" Connor shouted. "You're not going to do this to me!" First he was yelling at the sky, then toward the hole in the water. "You're not going to do this to me!"

"He'll know to back himself out," I called, hoping, even as the question—*What if he can't find the opening?*—numbed my thinking. But half a second later Uncle Ben splashed up through the surface of the water and began grabbing at the ice nearest him.

Ice that broke away.

"Hang on, Uncle Ben!" Connor called to him. "We're coming!"

We drove our machines out as far as we thought the ice would allow and then made our way the rest of the distance to the edge of the hole on our hands and knees.

Uncle Ben wasn't yelling, which was good. He'd need the energy later.

"Brenna," Connor said, "you go to the edge and grab his hands. I'll pull you."

"All right." It sounded risky and like it could never work. But we didn't have a lot of time to play with. The cold and the weight of Uncle Ben's soaked clothes would be working against us. We had to try something. We were in the middle of Mike Leothke's property, and nobody was going to happen along to help us.

"Take my hands!" I called to Uncle Ben.

He did, just as Connor grabbed hold of my legs and started to pull.

But the ice . . . it began to squeal and pop underneath me like twisting and tearing plastic. It wasn't going to hold.

"Pull her back, Connor!" Uncle Ben let go of my hands.

"No!" But Uncle Ben was splashing in the water again, and Connor was yanking me back to safer ice. "Connor, we can't just—"

"The rope!"

"What?"

"The rope on the back of your snowmobile!"

Understanding, I got to my feet and ran. My hands seemed asleep as I fumbled with the rope around the cooler on the back of my snowmobile. It had been wound around itself so many times that I was afraid I was only tangling it instead of getting it loose. But it did come loose, and I tossed one end of it to Connor.

"Grab this, Uncle Ben, and loop it around yourself!" Connor tossed it out over the water. "Brenna, tie your end of it tight around your seat."

"I'm on it."

"We're going to use the snowmobile to pull you up, Uncle Ben!"

I tied the rope as securely as I could get it, jumped onto my seat, and started the engine.

Behind me, Uncle Ben managed to get the rope around him, but he was breathless and still splashing against chunks of ice that offered him nothing. "Connor . . . I can't . . . tie it."

"That's all right. Just hang on!"

"Connor," I yelled back to him, "his hand. He won't be able to—"

In my brother's eyes in the fraction of a second that he looked at me, I saw fear. And anger. "He has to! Now go!"

I squeezed the throttle as hard as it would go and drove. In glances over my shoulder, I saw Connor running behind me, away from the ice breaking all around Uncle Ben as he was dragged into, through, and past it. I felt the strain in the snowmobile's engine and worried about its ability to pull Uncle Ben up once he hit ice that wouldn't break. But only vaguely. All I was thinking about was driving.

Soon there was a rough jerk on the machine, and I looked back to see Uncle Ben on solid ice again.

I kept driving. He wouldn't mind being dragged a little ways, I was sure, to get off the ice.

I stopped the snowmobile near the first tree I came to and ran back to where Uncle Ben was lying on the ground. He was shivering, and struggling to catch his breath, but his eyes were open, and he was saying something to me.

"What?" I leaned close to him.

"Nice driving." He lifted his hand to wipe at the tears on my cheek. "It's okay."

"I thought you were going to die," I said.

Connor ran up behind me. "Don't waste time talking, Bren," he said. "We've got to get him warm." And he was all business. Getting Uncle Ben out of his wet clothes. Putting his own snow pants, gloves, and jacket on him, not that they fit. Helping him onto the seat behind me on my snowmobile. Telling me to head for the cabin and that he'd catch up. His snowmobile was still out on the pond.

"The cabin's right at the bottom of this pass," I promised Uncle Ben as I started down the trail. I really wasn't sure how much farther down the pass the cabin was, but I knew he'd need to believe that he wasn't going to be this cold for too much longer.

I had to drive more slowly than I would have liked because Uncle Ben was a little unsteady on the seat behind me, and Connor caught up with me soon. When he pulled around and past us, I saw that he was shivering without his snow gear. And that he was crying.

"I'll go ahead and get some more wood in the fire," he yelled back to me without looking over his shoulder.

He must have thrown in half the woodpile, I thought, as I helped Uncle Ben past the cabin door and to the chair that Connor had pulled right up next to the woodstove. The place was offensively warm.

Perfect.

"You're going to be okay, now, Uncle Ben." Connor sat beside him and handed him a mug of something steaming. "It's tea," he said. "Drink it."

Uncle Ben nodded and wrapped his hands gratefully around the mug.

"Do you want some?" Connor asked me.

"I'll get it."

"Connor," Uncle Ben said after we'd been sitting there a while, "Brenna, you two really kept your heads out there. I'm proud of you."

"I . . . you weren't going to die," Connor said. "That's all. You weren't going to die." He looked away from Uncle Ben. "I told myself when I first got here that I wasn't going to care. Because I cared about Mom and Dad and they left me. But then, when you got shot, I . . . I did care. You can't leave us. Brenna and me. You're all we've got."

Uncle Ben placed his hand on Connor's arm and waited for him to look at him again. "Is that what you've been thinking all this time?"

Connor nodded. "Yes. I mean, Brenna and I have each other, and Aunt Esther, but—"

"The truth is, Connor," Uncle Ben said, holding up his hand to interrupt him, "something could happen to me. The past couple of months are proof of that. Something could happen to any one of us. To Brenna. Or Nathan. Or . . . or Esther." He squinted his eyes against the heat coming at him from the stove and worked to steady his breathing. He was still shivering. "All that any one of us has guaranteed at any moment in our lives is God, that moment, the people in it, and His promises."

"Well . . . okay." Connor stood up and reached for the empty mug in Uncle Ben's hand. "But you weren't going to die."

Chapter 22

I accepted the platter of roast beef from Tony Kramer and put two slices on my plate before passing it on to Connor. It was Easter, and Uncle Ben and Aunt Esther had once again invited a mob for dinner. The Kramers. The Teales. The Cahills. The Rubys—Jimmy and his parents. Rachel and Judah were home, of course, and Rachel had brought her roommate with her. Stella, whose parents were in Hawaii for the week. There were more people seated around the table than it was meant to accommodate, but nobody seemed the least bit put out by the lack of elbow room.

Easter had never been a big event in our family, but I had still braced myself for some of what Uncle Ben called The Holiday Roller Coaster. It had come, but not to the degree that it had at Christmas, and I was relieved—and a little surprised—to be enjoying the day.

Really enjoying it.

Uncle Ben had preached a short but convincing sermon about the difference between living life and just having it. On each of the three Sundays since our snowmobiling trip, I'd made a deliberate effort to pay attention to the things that were happening around me at church. The words to the songs we sang. The things people said to one another in the entryway before and after the service. The sermon.

Uncle Ben had said at the cabin that a person could only be sure of four things.

THE WAY OF ESCAPE

God.

The moment he was living.

The people in that moment.

God's promises.

Those words had refused to leave me alone in the van on our way back. I'd been sitting in the front passenger seat, theoretically helping Uncle Ben stay awake since we hadn't been able to leave the cabin until after midnight because it had taken him that long to warm up.

"Were you scared?" I'd asked him.

"Under the ice?" He'd nodded. "Oh, yeah. See, I knew the way out was right there, but I'd gotten turned around. I'm banging up on the ice, knowing that if I don't find that hole soon, or break through a new one, I'm going to run out of life. So, yeah, I was scared. But then it was there."

We had talked more after that, but when I started babbling on about the family relationships of chimpanzees—something we'd just studied in school, not that I cared—he laughed and assured me that he was fine and I didn't need to talk just to talk. He'd slept at the cabin, so he wasn't sleepy.

I kept myself awake, thinking. Just to be sure Uncle Ben stayed fine . . . and because he'd given me a lot to think about.

See, I knew the way out was right there.

I'm going to run out of life.

Could it be that that's what I had been doing? Running out of life? Not just since my parents' death, but all along? With the answer—the way out, the promised way of escape that Uncle Ben had told me about so long ago—right there?

People found security, or what they thought of as security, in all kinds of things. Other people. Money. Their position in society. In themselves and their abilities. But at any moment, any one or all of those things could be taken away or changed or invalidated.

It had happened to me.

But it wasn't the same with God.

He was the constant. The one thing in the universe that would not change or go away or lose His importance.

And I was basically clueless about Him. Yes, I knew He was and that His Son had died on the cross to provide for my salvation and that He had a role in our lives . . .

But, suddenly, that night in the van, that wasn't good enough for me anymore. There was more to God than that. Much more. And I wanted to know it. To know Him.

So I'd started to pay attention at church. And to ask Uncle Ben about some of the things I didn't understand when I read the Bible. And to pray to God as if He could and would really hear and answer, not just because I knew I should.

My parents were dead. Well, they weren't alive on earth anymore. I'd always have and treasure my memories of the moments I'd had with them . . . but I was still living. On earth. Moment by moment by moment.

God. The moment. The people in it. His promises.

Uncle Ben and Aunt Esther were not, and never could be, my parents. But they loved me. This house that I was eating Easter dinner in wasn't my house, but it was all the home I'd have from now on. Rachel's room was beginning to feel more and more like my room every day. I'd hung the picture Tony had given me, along with several others that I'd taken out of my scrapbook and framed. Pictures of Montana. Pictures of Mom and Dad. Pictures of Connor and me. A picture of Shadow, Grandpa's big black horse. A picture of Uncle Ben and me that Connor had taken at Mr. Leothke's cabin before we'd gotten on the snowmobiles that morning. And one of Aunt Esther and me walking out the door together on the morning of Bring Your Parents to School Day.

When Tony Kramer passed the bowl of mashed potatoes to me, I smiled at him. He wasn't a close friend, but he was becoming one. "Thanks," I told him.

"You bet."

After scooping some potatoes onto my plate, I passed the bowl to Connor. He, too, had been changed by that snowmobiling trip. The two of us had actually talked about Mom's and Dad's deaths for the first time, and we had made a pact to be there for one another. Whatever the time. Whatever the need. And he'd promised to be more tolerant of my crying. In fact, he'd done a bit of it himself. He still didn't participate in our fairly regular around-the-dinner-table conversations about God, but he'd begun to pay attention to them and to ask me questions about them when we were alone.

He passed the potatoes on to Dr. Teale without taking any. There was no more room on his plate.

"Excuse me," someone said. It was Judah. He pushed his chair back slowly and stood up. "I want to say something."

I noticed Stephanie whisper to Nathan, who glanced across the table at Rebekah and then grinned. He picked up his fork and knife and did a gentle drum roll with them on the edge of his plate.

"Knock it off," Judah told him. "This is serious."

Nathan laughed. "And a complete mystery, I'm sure."

Someone started humming the tune to "The Wedding March."

Another voice joined in.

Judah looked at Rebekah. She could only shrug.

"All right, then, sing," he said. "But keep it down."

Rebekah turned toward her mother and covered her mouth with her hand. That hid the smile but not the fact that she was smiling. Her eyes gave her away.

"I can see that this isn't going to come as a surprise to any of you," Judah said. "But—"

Another drum roll from Nathan.

Judah ignored it. "As of yesterday, it's official."

The rest of his announcement couldn't be heard above our excited response, but Rebekah didn't hesitate to punctuate whatever it was he was saying by holding out her left hand for all of us to see.

I looked at the ring, waited for Judah to look my way, which he seemed to do right away, and smiled at him. He had done a good job. The ring was beautiful. And so was Rebekah.

"The date?" Aunt Esther wanted to know once the congratulations had started to quiet down.

"A year from August," Judah said.

"We want both of you to do the ceremony," Rebekah said to her father and Uncle Ben. "Pastor Ewen, you can do the message and the actual 'I now pronounce you man and wife' thing, and Dad, you can do the vows and the unity candle and—"

"She's not excited, or anything, is she?" Connor leaned toward me to whisper.

I smiled at him. "Maybe just a little."

"Well," he said, "she couldn't have picked a better family to get into."

I nodded. "That's for sure."